D1743295

Three Tales of Vampires

I:
Murderous Little Darlings

II:
The Blood and the Raven

III:
Innocent While She Sleeps

© 2015

John Hennessy

Dedication

Aditi Saha – for seeking out my first fiction novel, *Dark Winter*, amongst the millions of books out there, and believing in me from the start.

Merril Anil – your sharp wit and critical reviews always make me become a better writer.

Adriana Girolami – for your unwavering support and always getting the word out about my books – thank you.

With special thanks to my mother, Mary Hennessy, who reads all of my books.

Also dedicated to anyone who has come through dark periods in their life, somehow finding the resolve to overcome the difficulties life throws at them. The mind really is more powerful than we think.

First published in the United Kingdom in 2015.

Text copyright © John Hennessy 2015
The right of John Hennessy to be identified as the author of this work is asserted by him.

ISBN-13: 978-1514117163 (CreateSpace-Assigned)
ISBN-10: 1514117169

A CIP Catalogue record for this book is available from the British Library.

This is a work of fiction. Names, characters, places, incidents, and dialogues are products of the author's imagination or are used fictitiously. Any resemblance to actual people, living or dead, events or locales is entirely coincedental.

Praise for
The Tales of Vampires Series

"I loved the humour in the dialogue and young adults, in fact any reader will love it. It isn't too graphic and the story has left me wanting to read more." – *Sharon Brownlie*

"While each book had been dealing with a single separate story, a common string has been following from the very first book in all three of them. Like the previous two books, the story flips and does a strong 360 on you at the very end, which you have least expected and this only adds to the craving for the next book." – *Merril Anil*

"The story line is so appealing and easy to read, but still gives you chill and those cliff-hangers keep you engaged wanting to know what come next." – *Adriana Girolami*

"Do read this book, if you want to experience fear in a whole new level." – *Aditi Saha*

"I am now almost sold on the whole idea of vampires, if the stories could all be this slick and funny." – *Lesley Hayes*

"John has a way with words that appeals to me and what I like most in his plots is that I can't discover what is happening until the end, when he reveals everything to the readers." – *Cristiane Serruya*

"This is not your typical vampire story, John has created a fascinating world, that I imagine gets even more incredible with each installment." – *Christian Green*

Murderous Little Darlings

First Kill

With two specimens of the undead either side of her, Juliana knew there was no escape. Kill the one they had selected for her, or *be* killed, and become one of them. What had the neighbours in the road called them, back when their childhood pranks were just that? Eggs thrown at the front door, maybe a small stone hurled at a window. Nothing major. No biggie. Nothing to write home about.

That was until the stones got larger, and one, hurled through a window, cracked Old Nellie Hall's skull right open, right in front of her grandchildren. On her 90th birthday, no less.

Protecting his young sister, Marcus admitted it was his fault, even though Juliana had thrown the rock, albeit under duress from her brothers.

Oh yes, she remembered what the locals called them now. *Murderous Little Darlings.* They had the faces of angels, but possessed the very souls of the Devil. Their mother's human existence ended the moment she had been made one of the undead. She, in turn, had died giving birth to them. Marcus had fully embraced his vampire side from the moment he was born. He was the oldest of the triplets by a full hour.

Rocco was the second eldest, and had fought the temptation all of his life. Then one day, Marco finally broke him.

That just left Juliana.

Despite her protestations to the contrary, Marcus told her that *We are what we are, and we do what we do.* But Marcus was just six years old when he made his first kill, a Mr Eric Mitchell, who was eighty-seven years old at the time of death. The marks on his neck healed up instantly once Marcus had drunk his fill. At six years of age, who could possibly point the finger at Marcus? In any case, as Marcus put it, *'At eighty-seven years old, whatever you died of, it's natural causes anyway.'*

The very next day, Marcus put a football through an open garage door, knocking over Mr Hill.

"You little devil," he screamed. "When I get hold of you, I'll *murder* you."

"Not if I get you first," Marcus retaliated.

So as not to arouse suspicion, Marcus left it a week. Then, taking Rocco along with him, he woke Mr and Mrs Hill whilst they slept in their beds, and bludgeoned them both with a mallet almost too big for them to hold in their hands.

"Do it now, Rocco, sink your teeth in hard before they die. They weren't much use in life to anyone anyway, and – what the hell is this? Where do you think you're going?"

Mrs Hill had escaped from her bed and ran down the stairs screaming, clutching the back of her head to stop her brains from falling out.

"Rocco, take him good. I'll go after *her.*"

Rocco pinned Mr Hill down. It was easy, because the old man was paralysed with fear. With his brother chasing a frantic Mrs Hill to her doom, Rocco paused. It hurt when he had bitten people before. His fangs weren't fully formed, although Marcus promised that with each kill, they would get stronger.

Okay. There was time to do this. Rocco leaned back, bared his teeth, and sank them into Mr Hill's throat. The contact wasn't all that great, and bits of hair from Mr Hill's neck found their way between the gaps in Rocco's mouth. It wasn't a good taste. Rocco didn't understand or truly share his older brother's bloodlust. But if he didn't do the job properly, Mr Hill would die an even more unpleasant death.

So Rocco wrapped a small arm around Mr Hill's neck and placed the bite as hard as he could. The skin punctured better this time, just as Marcus promised it would. Marcus was always right.

Rocco drank his fill, the taste of so much blood all at once leaving him dizzy, and Mr Hill limply collapsed on the bed, his outstretched hands almost touching the floor. Rocco did feel a pang of remorse, then scratched the thought from his head. Such thoughts would make Marcus angry. And you wouldn't want to make Marcus angry.

There they were, Mr Hill, now the extremely deceased Mr Hill in one corner of the room, Rocco, just days before his seventh birthday, in the other. He sucked his thumb like he was a toddler once more, as it gave him some comfort.

Downstairs, Marcus could be heard crashing into things. Or maybe he was crashing Mrs Hill into things. To Marcus, such details weren't important. The big details, such as the hunt, and the eventual kill, that was all that mattered.

Rocco sucked harder on his thumb as the crashes got louder. He didn't like the wails and screams from Mrs Hill, who was begging for her life. Marcus did enjoy the victim's futile attempts to save themselves, even though the outcome was always the same.

"They struggle when you hold them down, and maybe, sometimes they get away from you, but not for long, and they never, *ever* live to tell who and what hunted them. There's something else in our favour too, little brother. The world just doesn't believe in vampires."

"You're sure?" inquired Rocco, a desperate expression on his face. "I mean, you're absolutely sure of this? We're *vampires*? We have to feed on humans to survive?"

Marcus shook his head, unable to mask his disappointment in his brother. "Your brain deserves to exist in a better body than yours, Rocco. My, what a dreary way to describe our existence. No! We feed on humans to *live*! You should embrace the life, as I do, brother!"

Rocco just didn't get the same sense of joy that Marcus got from killing. He wasn't alone in thinking like that, and yet, Rocco sensed that his sister Juliana would soon be coerced to join in *the life*.

His thoughts were shattered by a piercing shout from downstairs. "Rock! Get your thumb out of your ass and get down here now!"

Rocco collected himself from the heap on the floor and, frantic as he was to get downstairs, he knocked over a photo on the bed stand of a young couple, perhaps the Hills' children. He'd know for sure soon enough if they ever came looking.

"My thumb wasn't in my ass."

"Might have well have been," said Marcus. "Or perhaps you were sucking on your thumb again, like the *ickle baybee* that you are."

"Don't call me that," said Rocco. "I'm older than *Julie*."

"Yeah, well, you had better starting acting like you're older than *Joo-lee*, otherwise....well...you know the consequences."

Time and again, Juliana had disobeyed Marcus' order to join them on the hunt. For this latest act of defiance, she was locked in the wardrobe, and had been in there for two whole days. Rocco, terrified of enclosed spaces *and* his brother, agreed to go on the night's hunt in her place.

Mrs Hill whimpered on the floor, and Marcus lightly kicked her body with kicks regular-as-clockwork.

"Is she going to die?" asked Rocco.

"Hmmph!" grunted Marcus. "I suppose you think she was actually living? No, brother, she's already dead. Husband barely recognises her or himself, and the kids, especially the grandkids, they never visit. She may be breathing, but she's been dead a long time, actually. We're just taking care of the nasty side of business. I find this such a thankless task. No-one will ever understand our work on this Earth."

Rocco wanted to say that he could not drink anymore, but by doing so, Marcus would force Juliana into the *game*. Although being locked in the wardrobe used to be a game, it was now more of a punishment. Rocco had been placed in solitary confinement once before, and he was so delirious with hunger he fed on the first thing his bleary eyes lay sight on. From that day on, Marcus had convinced Rocco that he was a vampire.

The dizzy hit from the blood of Mr Hill told its own story. Marcus did what he always did, and took the situation into his own hands.

Walking across the road to their home, which was surrounded by tall gunmetal gates, their foundations buried deep in the ground, he walked up the stairs to one of the unused bedrooms, and unlocked the wardrobe door, the top of which was almost three times his own height.

"Juliana? Julie?"

No answer. Marcus felt his heart quicken, uncomfortable with the anguish he may have caused her. Had she been left on her own for far too long?

"Julie? Joo-leee!!"

Marcus stood back from the wardrobe and surveyed the darkness. He observed some scratch marks on the inside the door, and with closer inspection, he could make out what could only be Juliana's fingernails embedded in the wood. The flaky bits of nail could not have belonged to Rocco, because he always bit his nails down to the stub.

"Juliana?"

Somewhere, amidst the darkness that had taken up happy residence within the wardrobe, a bloody hand grabbed at Marcus' neck and pulled him inside. He was thrown at breakneck speed towards the back of the wardrobe, and only stopped when his head connected hard, dulling his senses on impact.

He knew the wardrobe was huge. He'd spent time with Rocco playing *the game* but it would always be safe as one of them would be on the outside whilst the other was locked on the inside. In those playful times, the heart would quicken as the last sliver of light disappeared, and the door would slam shut. For added effect, Rocco would turn the key in the lock, and with it, would disappear any chance of escape for Marcus.

In the darkness which enveloped him like a shroud, along with the silence that joined it in happy unison, he would wait. Of course, the first plea to be let out would be ignored. That was part of the game. The second plea would be ignored too, even though Rocco could hear the banging.

That too, was part of the game. Although for Marcus, the length of time between the first set of bangs and the second became more uncomfortable, to the point that he informed Rocco that *he* would be the one playing the game if the rules were not adhered to. Of course, these rules were the kind that Marcus dictated, and could change at any time.

Rocco had agreed, because there was no disagreeing with Marcus. After a pre-agreed period of time, the lock would make that reassuring clicking sound, and Marcus would be free. Then Rocco would take his place in the dark, never-ending wardrobe. Marcus always said the time was the same, but it wasn't. He'd keep Rocco in there just that little while longer. After all, time has no meaning in the dark.

This time though, he had misjudged things terribly. He knew Juliana would be unnerved, perhaps to the point of a heightened sense of terror. But he just wanted to teach her a lesson, that's all.

Now, it was he who found himself locked in the wardrobe. The turn of the key had been decisive. Juliana was seriously pissed off. The force with which she ripped the key from the lock made the hair stand up on the back of his neck.

She'd come back soon though. She wouldn't leave him in there indefinitely.
Surely?

Beyond the confines of his imprisonment, there was complete silence. On those previous occasions where they had played the game, Marcus had noticed how the air was literally sucked out of that space once the door was closed. Rocco had mentioned it too, but it didn't seem so terrifying back then.

Okay. So Juliana wasn't going to answer. Marcus had to hope that Rocco would at least come to the aid of his brother.

It was hard to tell with any certainty how much time had passed, but Marcus decided he had had enough, and banged, kicked, shunted the wardrobe for all he was worth. The wardrobe refused to budge.

"Piss!!!!" screamed Marcus. "I will piss all over you when I get hold of you Julie!"

He sank to his knees, before experiencing a moment of clarity. The Dark One could do it. After all, he had the power. He was the one who gave them the power in the first place. The one who made them.

"Dark Lord, I serve you in all and everything. I ask only for the freedom to do your will."

Silence.

"I will sacrifice Juliana for you. She will not become one of the undead. I will commend her soul to the black earth."

The door unlocked, and Marcus smiled. He wanted to scream out *Oh Julie? I'm coming for you* but they were a bit old for games of hide and seek. He would find her, get the body of Mrs Hill, and Juliana could feed on her. If not, Marcus decided he would feed on her. On his own sister, no less.

You shouldn't have locked me in, Julie. Now look what you've made me do.

***

"Come on Rocco. We're going," said Juliana.

"But Marcus will be after us," pleaded Rocco. "He'll find us, and when he does, he'll kill us."

"He won't kill his own brother and sister. No matter what he's capable of, I won't believe he would do that."

Juliana was wrong. Marcus was very capable, and was capable of doing anything. Juliana had explained that Marcus was now locked in the wardrobe, but Rocco didn't believe that meant he would be contained in it for long.

Juliana simply didn't believe Marcus was a vampire, much less herself. *He's a bloody psychopath, that's what he is,* she told Rocco one time, who keep shushing her because of Marcus' super-sensitive vampire hearing.

"Come *on,* Rocco. Otherwise I will leave you with Marcus. I'm not having any part of this madness."

Rocco grabbed his sister by the arm. He was older than her, but he knew he was the troublesome *middle* sibling, neither the eldest nor the youngest, and hardly ever listened to.
Marcus had convinced him that he was a vampire. Perhaps Juliana just hadn't developed the taste for it yet. But he had to ask her, all the same.

"Julie, don't you ever…don't you ever get the urge? I mean, an irresistible urge to satisfy the bloodlust? I do. I really do. I have fought it, but as their bodies lay downstairs, I just wanted to rip them apart, you know?"

Juliana paused before answering. She knew that time was against them, that Marcus was coming, and yes, he would be super-pissed off. As her hormones had begun to rearrange parts of her body, she knew the anger they gave her would be small change compared to what Marcus' level of rage would be. No, she didn't believe Marcus was a vampire. But she did believe in his powers of persuasion. A vulnerable child like Rocco would be easily persuaded. If Marcus said he was a vampire, then he was a vampire. If he told Rocco that he was a vampire too, then he was a vampire.

He'd told Juliana that she was the same, the 'siblings of bloodlust', he had named them.

"We're not," she retorted. "I won't give into that *living death*."

Juliana and Rocco raced to the door, but a shadow confronted them as they made it to the bottom of the stairs.

"It's okay," said Marcus. "I forgive you, Juliana. I forgive you. First kills are the hardest. I understand why you got upset."

Juliana and Rocco breathed heavily and deeply, trying to get their blood pressure down.

"So you're not going to harm us?" asked Rocco.

Marcus shook his head. "Of course not, brother. I need you. I need all of us to stay true to each other."

"Mrs Hill." Juliana's words punctured the air like a pick breaking up ice.

"Dead as a rat, caught by a cat," he sang. "Tasted kinda crusty. You didn't miss much."

"What did you do with the body?"

"Don't worry about that. We'll find someone suitable to your palate. A sixteen-year-old virgin, perhaps."

Being killed by Marcus, or taking the vampire's kiss, thus making her undead; neither status appealed to Juliana.

I forgive you, Marcus had told her. But if she never killed anyone in his presence, and more specifically, failed to look like she was enjoying it, he would never forgive her.

Juliana was shocked that Marcus made no reference to the wardrobe, nor showed any remorse over the killing of the Hills. Most of all, she knew he would never stop until she had finally given into the bloodlust in the same carnal manner her brother enjoyed.

Juliana knew what she must do. In that moment, she realised with horror that Marcus would have to die.

Grave Error

Cemeteries were usually quiet, reverent places. Still others might say that cemeteries were spooky, and what business would the living have, walking amongst the dead. Marcus, for one, would never say they were spooky; and on this point at least, Juliana found herself agreeing with her brother.

"They are, however, the best places to find new blood," announced Marcus. "Even better when there's a crowd of them, like a hundred or so. Usually, when there's a new plot dug, the funeral party finds itself in close proximity to another freshly dug grave. That's when you grab one of the party, give them your kiss, and no-one notices until they've got back home. By then, it's too late."

Juliana thought the whole idea was grotesque. There was no honour in killing in that way. But Marcus never squared up to anyone bigger than himself, at least....not when they were awake. Suddenly, she found herself speaking out loud.

"This whole thing is gross, and utterly barbaric. You are a coward, Marcus."

Fully expecting Marcus to rage at her, Juliana expressed mild surprise when he didn't seem to get annoyed by her statement.

"Well?"

"I just don't understand you two," said Marcus, sighing like Juliana had said the most awful thing in the world. "It's a hell of thing, killing someone. You'll see the light extinguish from their eyes – now that's the last thing to leave their so-called life. Your teeth buried into their neck is the last thing they feel, and you'll be the last thing they'll see. You take all they are, all they were, and all they will ever be. The vampire's kiss is the most efficient of killing tools. One bite takes all."

"It's gross. Barbaric. And utterly needless."

"If they are deserving, we give them a *new* life, Joolee."

"And if not, they die. Just because you say so."

"Not me! The one who made us what we are."

Juliana tried to stand up, but Marcus sprang up beside her. "No," he said. "You cannot let them see you. Not yet."

They counted twenty cars in all that came over the brow of the hill. Marcus motioned that the younger people were usually in the cars to the rear, and that whilst the adults usually kept the children in front of them at the graveside, there were always some who bored easily and wandered off.

Sure enough, as the service began, one child, of about fifteen, snuck out from underneath the arms of his parents, and started playing a game on his phone.

The eleven-year-old Marcus positioned himself between the older boy, his phone, and a newly dug hole to the left of him. Marcus bared his teeth. The older boy did his best to keep a straight face.

"Oh. You're a vampire?"
"Yes."

"So what does that make me, your victim?"

"You're clearly not as dumb as you look."

The older boy pushed Marcus back. "Oh fuck off."

Some of the adults from the service turned around and 'hushed' at the boy.

"See my sister over there?" Marcus inquired. "She's a vampyric virgin. To a lay person like you, that means she has yet to feed on someone. Might as well be you. Watch your swearing though, you'll offend her delicate sensibilities."

Taking the mick out of Marcus, the boy spoke in a mock Oxfordshire tone. "Then I will speak in a tone more agreeable to her ears."

"We're at a funeral, not some Jane Austen regency period drama where you're the fucking dandy."

"Ash!" hissed one of the adults. "*Ashley*. Get over here and stop messing around with that phone. Pay your respects!"

"Ashley?!" laughed Marcus. "You've got a fucking girl's name, Ashley? Pardon me, we clearly are in a Jane Austen novel. I suppose you would like a pelisse to go with your *hat*."

The adults turned back, clearly expecting their orders to be followed. Marcus took his chance and launched himself at Ashley, knocking him into the open grave.

The gathered, who were in prayer paid no attention to the commotion behind them. Ashley would have screamed, only the fall appeared to have knocked him out cold. Marcus ran back to Juliana, and told her that she could do the deed now, or join Ashley in the hole.

The conversation went on at whisper level behind the largest of the gravestones, an angel with head bowed, holding a crucifix in her hands. Juliana stalled for time, but it seemed even being in public view wasn't going to stop Marcus. He chastised Rocco for saying nothing, and jabbed his finger into his shoulder.

"You're supposed to be doing this stuff too, you know. Now put on Ashley's hat and make yourself useful. Go stand by the mourners."

Marcus picked up Ashley's fallen hat, and jammed it onto Rocco's head. "There. You look like a sad sack of a fuck, just like Ashley there. Do it before he wakes up."

Marcus spun Rocco around by his shoulders, and pushed him in the direction of the group. Juliana looked at Rocco, who must have been a good six inches shorter in height than Ashley. Marcus was betting that the group wouldn't notice. Juliana's view unsurprisingly differed, and believed that the subterfuge wouldn't last.

"*Now*, Julie."

Juliana continued to stall for time. Peering into the grave, she could see that Ashley had been knocked cold from the fall. Marcus was so strong for his age, and his height. Could it be true? Could he really be a vampire? She knew that vampires had strength often ten times the strength of normal humans. Marcus, for his part, certainly lacked no self-belief. In his head, he was a vampire, and every day, he lived and breathed a vampire existence.

To feed on another human…even the mere thought of the act, disgusted her. Whilst she paused, he grabbed her arm and pulled her into the open grave. He gestured to the stricken Ashley, and ordered her to feed on him.

Juliana rebuked him. Exasperated, Marcus spoke gently to Juliana, whilst at the same time grabbing the boy's ankle, exposing his fresh skin. Making gnawing sounds and smiling at his sister, he dropped the leg, which made a clunking sound on the soft ground.

"It's not that bad, really. Tastes pretty much the same like pork." He made burping sounds which disgusted Juliana, and she went to climb out of the hole in which she found herself. Marcus grabbed her leg.

"Don't make me do it to you, sis. Come on now. *Feed.*"

Juliana kicked out and scrambled out of the hole. She ran towards the group of people, which by now had realised Rocco was not who he was supposed to be. At the same time, a blood- curdling scream was heard from the grave. Ashley's mother ran to the open grave, and screamed herself when she saw Marcus ripping into Ashley, who appeared to be conscious whilst it was happening.

Several men from the group surrounded the grave and pulled Marcus away from Ashley, who was bleeding heavily, but alive. Marcus was delirious and thrashed about wildly as two men - then four, held him down. Finally, six men subdued him, and he stopped fighting them.

A phone call to the police and an ambulance had already been made, and soon, Marcus found himself in handcuffs, whilst Ashley, who was suffering from shock and a minor loss of blood, was lifted into the ambulance.

Juliana grabbed Rocco and together, they ran as fast as they could. If the other people could have seen them, surely they would have subdued them as well. With her heart belting out of her chest, Juliana wished that just for that moment, that they actually were vampires, and could escape detection. It would only be a matter of time before they were caught.

Now You See Me

Marcus sat in the interview room, wearing a bemused smile on his face when he thought he was being watched. It would fall from his face when a police officer would come into the room. It was a well-practiced routine that police were used to, but not with someone so young.

Finally, the officer spoke.

"You are here because you assaulted another person. You then proceeded to bite him, drawing blood from his leg. You had accomplices too. If you tell us where they were going, we can co-operate with you."

He clapped his notebook to a close. "Now. Where are they?"

"Why don't you ask me who *I* am?," asked Marcus calmly. "Or is it the case that you don't know? Did my fingerprints turn up nothing?"

The police officer, a man in his forties, had been in the force for twenty years. He had never dealt with a situation like this before. No, the fingerprints had turned up nothing. Neither had the swab test. It was as if Marcus didn't exist. But then, why would he have a criminal record?

"We know that you have a sister and a brother. We know that you are a seriously disturbed individual. And we know that you have no parents."

"My fingerprints told you all that?"

The police officer did all he could not to lunge at Marcus. Then, the door to the interview room opened, and a female officer beckoned him to leave the room.

"I'm losing here. I hope you've got something."

"I do," she said. "Turns out he killed an old couple in their beds. Bashed their heads in with a hammer."

"What? You have proof?"

"Witness reports. Nothing concrete."

"Unbelievable. Any history of mental illness? I don't want them getting off on a technicality."

"You're going to love this. The duty officer asked him how old he was, and his reply was:- "

'I've been around for as long as I can remember. You see, I'm a vampire.'

"You're fucking kidding me."

"As God is my witness. Not that our boy knows anything about that. He has killed, Kelly. We just have to find a way to pin it on him."

Officer Kelly turned towards the observation window, which of course was only viewable one way.

"He doesn't look big enough to hold a hammer, never mind use it."

"Know anything about vampires?"

"Yeah. They're not real."

"How do you think something becomes real, Kelly? My mum suffered an aneurysm. So did you, back in the day. But up until I heard that word, I just thought she was having headaches. It becomes real. He thinks he's a vampire. It's real to him, and he will make it real to us."

"What are you suggesting, O'Hara? That I wear cloves of garlic around my neck?"

"Just treat him seriously, that's all."

Kelly mulled over O'Hara's words, then went back into the interview room.

"So you're a vampire? Is that the reason for all this madness, Marcus?"

"It's you who say that I am."

"So you're not a vampire?"

"It is *you* who says that I am." Marcus spoke far slowly, more deliberately.

"Let me say this, then," said Kelly, who was struggling to keep his composure. "Vampires sleep in their coffins at night. I've seen

Dracula. I know what he does. It's getting late now. You'll be looking for a coffin right about now, won't you?"

"It must be a great comfort to you, to make fun of me. I wonder will you feel the same, once I feed on *you*."

"You don't scare me, kid. You talk like a cannibal, not a vampire. You are a killer. And we will pin the Hill murders on you. Make no mistake. All the breadcrumbs you guys leave always leave a trail."

"You're wrong, *Occifer*. I am not a killer. I am what I am. And I am not in the breadcrumb leaving business."

Kelly smiled with a well-worn sense of defeat. "Don't be so cryptic. Say what you mean."

Marcus smiled back at Kelly, before saying, "If you're going to follow in my footsteps, be sure to cover your tracks."

"Now what is *that* supposed to mean?"

"It means that you can keep me here, put me in a cell, restrict my freedom. But you won't be able to hold me. It means, no breadcrumbs."

"Because you're a vampire, right?"

"Because you're incompetent."

"Where's your parents?"

"In the ground. Six feet under, give or take an inch."

"Think you're funny, don't you?" Kelly knew he was taking the kid's bait, but couldn't help himself. True to form, Marcus responded in kind.

"You're the funny one, thinking you can actually keep me in here."

Kelly could feel the vein on his head throbbing, from an aneurysm he suffered in his twenties. This Marcus was trying to make it burst. *You've had a mild cerebral aneurysm, Mr Kelly,* the doctors had told him. He had told them they had a pretty fucked up idea of what mild was.

"Go on then. Escape."

"Why would I escape, when I can go of my own free will?" Marcus leaned in towards Kelly. "You haven't charged me with anything, *Occifer.*"

Kelly knew he hadn't charged Marcus with anything. But he had no intention of letting him go. He stood up, and announced he was going to get a coffee, that tonight was going to be a long night.

"You're leaving me here on my own?"

"No. O'Hara will deal with you."

"The white girl? Oh yes, do send her in, *Occifer*. English girls taste delicious."

More expletives emitted from Kelly, as Marcus continued to wind him up. The previously uncuffed child found his hands bound by steel, and Kelly clipped his legs to the chair for good measure.

Looking pleased with his restrain of the *little punk,* Kelly went to leave the interview room, safe in the knowledge that O'Hara could not be hurt. As he closed the door, through the window on the door he gave Marcus the V sign, and yet it was Marcus who won that last round, smacking his lips together. Kelly turned the room into darkness by killing the light.

As he turned around, his lips trembled; he was certain he could make out a set of glistening white fangs protruding from the boy's mouth.

Kelly, who was some thirty years older than O'Hara, placed a fatherly hand on her arm.

She smiled at him. "It's alright Kelly. What ever he has done, I'm not scared of him."

Kelly nodded, knowing that O'Hara could handle herself. After all, she had been the off-duty officer that had single handedly marched five armed gunmen out of a bank. Without a weapon.

For that act of bravery, she had been decorated, and was one of the most decorated officers in the police service.

Kelly realised he was sleepwalking towards retirement. But the killing of the Hills had disturbed him greatly, as it would disturb any sane, law-abiding citizen. Such people shouldn't have lived through wars to die so horribly. He had no compassion for the little punk. Slaps on the hand were all the kids got these days. The laws were weak, the politicians that made them were weak, making his job so much harder.

If kids like this one were not stopped, and were not stopped *now*, there would be no telling what they would do when they grew up.

All the same, Kelly knew a little about vampire lore; and vampires were not the kind of beings that grew up in those stories. Then there was the unsettling way Marcus thrashed about in the cemetery. It shouldn't have taken more than one officer, two at the most, to hold him down, cuff him, and read him his rights.

It had taken six.

Six.

"O'Hara, why don't you wait for me? I'm going to take a leak, then grab a coffee. Come with me. Leave Hannibal to stew a bit longer."

"Hannibal?"

"He's closer to the fictional Dr Lecter than the *Count*."

O'Hara wasn't fooled. She saw how Kelly had looked on leaving the interview room. Still, she had faced down those gunmen in the bank. She'd even done a tour of duty in Afghanistan as part of special operations. This kid was an anomaly, that was all.

Do send her in, Occifer. English girls taste delicious.

Why was this little bastard unsettling him so much?

"At least wait until I come back, O'Hara. Or take someone in with you."

O'Hara surmised it was just mind games that Kelly was playing, dismissed him with her hand, and opened the door.

At first, she said nothing to Marcus. She admitted to herself that there was something rather unsettling about him, and her own words to Kelly, about how *he thinks he's a vampire. It's real to him, and he will make it real to us.*
O'Hara let slip a little laugh. Marcus had read her like a book.

"Nervous are we, *Occifer*?"

"Why do you say it like that, when you know what you're saying. You know."

"Unsettles you, doesn't it?"

"Not in the slightest."

Marcus shrugged in his seat. "Now if you want me to tell the truth, you're going to have to start telling the truth. You can start with untelling that lie right now."

"Here's the truth," said O'Hara. "You're a vampire; at least you think you are. We know you have already killed some people, and they won't be your last victims. Your siblings have run out on you. When we catch them, and we will, they will squeal on you. Then, your killing days will be at an end. That's the truth."

"Truths are just lies, told with a confident smile on the face. And that is not just a truth, it's a fact."

"Is it indeed." It was spoken more as a statement than as a question from O'Hara, who took a swig from her bottle of still water.

"Blood is thicker than water," said Marcus.

"Are we reduced to digging up quotes now?"

"I hadn't finished," said Marcus. "Blood is thicker than water, and tastes better than water."

"That's not a saying."

"It is, around my way."

O'Hara was feeling exasperated, just as Kelly had been. Her older partner was taking his time, and this boy was unsettling her.

"Got any more sayings, from around your way?"

"Sure. You're all going to die tonight." Marcus paused slightly. "More of a statement of fact than an actual saying. Granted, it's not very catchy. But it's honest."

"You're not going to be able to back up that fact whilst you are in *those*." O'Hara pointed to the handcuffs.

Expecting Marcus to retort about the restraints, O'Hara was surprised to see Marcus position himself for a different response.

"He called you O'Hara. *Please*, tell me your first name is Scarlett." Marcus started to giggle, almost uncontrollably.

"My first name is of no consequence to you."

"I just like to know who I'm feeding on. A vampire never forgets the faces of those he has made anew."

"Interesting way to think of murder."

"You're not seeing the world through my eyes. But you will. We don't kill everyone. We make you anew. Why, you should embrace the life, as I do-"

Marcus broke off, the line he remembered telling his brother deeply disconcerted him.

"You weren't finished."

"Yes, I was."

There had to be a way to reach this kid. He didn't have the look of a killer, yet the evidence pointed to the facts. The Hills blood was on his hands, even if those same hands hadn't provided fingerprints to be matched to a database.

"What happened to your fingers, Marcus? Did you deliberately slice the skin off so that you wouldn't be detected? We know it was you. We know. There is nothing supernatural about you. You thinking you're a vampire doesn't make it so."

For once, Marcus refused to answer. After what seemed like an age, he spoke.

"We are what we think we are, not what others believe us to be. As for you, you are *Nina*. You look like a Nina. Definitely a vowel ending your name. You look like a Nina to me."

O'Hara tried not to look too stunned. She had seen these kind of illusions performed by mentalists. But he was right. Her first name *was* Nina. How the *little punk* knew her name, she did not know.

Was that fangs showing in his mouth? Ignoring his statement and instead intending to regain the initiative, she focussed on that instead.

"Open your mouth. Wide."

"Why?

"I think you know why."

"So come closer so you can have a look. *Nina*."

O'Hara got up so fast she nearly brought on a head rush. Marcus rattled the handcuffs at her.

"O'Hara!" barked a male voice curtly. "Leave him be."

Kelly had returned. He grabbed O'Hara by her wrist and pulled her out of the room.

"He knows my name, now how does he know that, Kelly? He can't know it, yet he does. I hope you've got something to pin the Hill murders to him, because….what?"

Kelly took a moment to look over O'Hara's shoulder.
The interview room was empty.

***

The police station was now a panic station, with everyone looking for the so-called little vampire. Marcus had disappeared, and more than that, had taken the handcuffs with him. The police rattled out the usual phrases, how *he couldn't have gotten far, be on the alert, shoot if absolutely (and bloody) necessary,* that sort of thing.

But for all Kelly's experience and O'Hara's decorations, the fact remained that an eleven-year-old boy, who may or may not be a vampire, had escaped.

"How do you think he did it, Kelly?"

"He's either a real vampire, with the strength of ten men, able to break his restraints, or he had something on him that helped him escape. Something he probably carries with him all the time now. I'd guess he was traumatised by some earlier life event, and doesn't want a repeat of it."

"So if it's the latter, how did he do it?"

"Probably a fan of Houdini. Maybe one of his fingers is fake, and carrying a pick, or something that would help him unlock something."
"We checked."

"Not nearly enough, apparently."

O'Hara knew Kelly was right, but couldn't help but be enraged by the implication. All the same, she interviewed him alone. She didn't wait for Kelly to return. Because of those decisions, now; if Marcus wanted to kill again, he was free to do so.

Her thoughts were broken by the shrill tone of her phone beeping. It was a text message from UNKNOWN that simply said:-

I've borrowed little Nina for a game you might know. Hide and Seek. Wanna play?

As she did, every weekday, Nina O'Hara had left her daughter at school, which was just two blocks away from the police station. How could Marcus have gotten there so fast? Had he really got to her daughter? She wanted to call *Little Nina,* but if Marcus had already gotten to her, it would need a different approach. O'Hara knew this. But her training had not prepared her for this eventuality.

Kelly knew O'Hara was beside herself with worry, so he tried to show his empathetic side. "We'll find him, and your little girl, okay, O'Hara?"

"What if he really is a vampire, Kelly? He'll kill her. I could have swore I saw fangs on him."

Kelly agreed, but not out loud. He didn't want O'Hara more spooked than she was already.

"Vampires don't kidnap, O'Hara." Kelly wanted to add something, but was unable to.

"They kill. That's what they do, Kelly. Oh my God, he's got my daughter, and he's going to kill her! We have to go!"

O'Hara went to run, but Kelly grabbed her arm. "Hey, I said we will find him. Your daughter will be found safe and -"

The lights in the police station all shut off at once. At first, they thought it was a power cut, but it became clear they were under attack. As gasps, shrieks and shouts could be heard all over the station, the lights came back on.

People stood around, wondering what had happened.

Then five corpses dropped from the platform above them, their bodies hitting the floor with a sickening crunch. On closer inspection, bite marks could be seen on the necks of the victims, and their chests had been ripped open, leaving bloody gaping holes. Five kills, exactly the same, and done in a matter of seconds, it seemed.

"Still think my daughter will be found safe, Kelly?"

O'Hara ran for the exit to the car park. She was through with observing protocol. What not thever force was needed to stop him, he had to be stopped. This vampire tale just got real.

On the Run

"**R**occo, you need to keep up with me. Damn it, why are   you

so slow?" Juliana could no longer run at her brother's pace, but he ran sluggishly, as if he didn't care.

"I'm not slow, just running at my own pace, which for me, is quite fast actually," he offered in reply. For Rocco, it was rather assertive of him. If it had been Marcus he had been talking to, he would have been shouted down; but Juliana wasn't like that.

Finally, he came to a full stop.

Juliana had been brushing by an array of people, some of which showed their annoyance to her by shouting 'bloody kids' as she passed them. To be fair to her brother, he had kept pace for a good while since leaving the cemetery, but as they had reached some countryside area, where few people seemed to be around, he took the chance to slow up.

"Some vampire you're supposed to be," barked Juliana. "We have to keep running, Rocco. We have to get far and away from here."

Rocco, who hadn't travelled much, only going as far as his brother would let him, had to smile. "Jooly, I don't even know where *here* is supposed to be."

Juliana brushed out her hair with both hands, turned around and placed her hands on her hips. Looking squarely at Rocco, she said, "It's just not far enough away. We have to keep running."

"Well, I've had enough of running," breathed Rocco, "and we should not have left Marcus to his fate. We are vampires, dear sis, and vampires don't run away. They kill what runs away."

Juliana sighed heavily. She had hoped that getting Rocco away from Marcus, that he would start to see sense; that Marcus was bad news, could not be placated. Juliana even recalled a previous conversation that the Hills had had with her, some weeks before Marcus killed them.

"You're his sister. He'd listen to you. He should go to the doctor and they would medicate him. He'd be alright if only he took his pills."

The only pill, the only drug that would help Marcus would be yet another kill. Juliana knew her brother looked angelic, and he had displayed many good personality traits, such as determination, mental toughness and honour. Yes, in Marcus' way of thinking, killing the Hills was an honourable thing to do.

However, the attack on the boy in full public view; was anything but honourable. Juliana didn't like being forced to do something she didn't want to do. And now they were on the run.

Finally, a pang of remorse bit at her. She started to believe that Rocco was right. They shouldn't have left Marcus to his fate. But he was killing not because he wouldn't stop – his core belief was that he was a vampire, and all killings were justified.
"It's like a cat killing a mouse," Marcus had once said. "That's the order of things."

Juliana could accept that argument; it was just that she just didn't like him forcing victims on her. If she ever was to *embrace the life*, it would be on her terms, and no-one else's. She did not like blood, hated flesh, despised killing. There had to be some kind of justification. She saw none.

"Okay," breathed Juliana. "Let's get a coffee and think this through."

They turned back on the country roads and back into the town. Looking as cute as a pair of buttons, Juliana and Rocco drew a lot of attention from onlookers, with *gasps* and *aww, aren't they cute* exclamations from a group of people that passed by them.

Juliana ordered two coffees and some rocky road cake, and sat them down by Rocco, who had been looking nervously outside of the coffee shop window.

Juliana gulped down the coffee, which tasted too good not to have an unsafe amount of sugar in it, whilst Rocco barely touched his cup.

"What is it, Rocco? Come on, the coffee's good here."

"I can't taste anything. Not since the Hill situation."

Juliana sympathised, and any pangs of remorse about leaving Marcus soon evaporated. Marcus could do what he wanted. He didn't have to rope Rocco into this game of his.

Trying his best to show gratitude to his sister, Rocco nibbled at the cake, but his facial expression could not betray his true feelings. To him, it had all the consistency of cardboard.

"You know sis, I didn't really believe Marcus, not at first. But he is committed to the life, and I'll admit I was fascinated at first. The reality is, I don't like it. Not after the Hills."

Juliana wanted to *shh* Rocco up, but knew that Marcus did this to his brother all the time. So she picked her next words with care.

"Maybe you can just tell me what you feel, without mentioning any names."

"I feel…we are in a lot of trouble. We can run, but not forever. The police will find us, and if they don't catch us first, our brother *will*."

"I won't let him harm you," said Juliana in a very sisterly manner, but looking at Rocco's sad face, she knew harm had already been done. "I'll get us another coffee, then we'll figure out what to do." Juliana took a napkin and smoothed out her brother's face; his cheeks burned red
and his eyes were all blood-shot and watery.

"Just a coffee," he said. "Not that I can really taste it."

Juliana mouthed an *okay* and patted her brother's hands.

***

Juliana returned with the cups of coffee, only for Rocco to gesture towards the tv screen high above him in the coffee house.

She could not advance further before the cups fell from her hands, and the hot liquid splashed against her legs. She did not scream, but gaped open mouthed at the screen, as the picture of Marcus appeared on the screen in the top right hand corner.

Running along at the bottom of the screen was the news ticker tape, which stated in white lettering on a red background

HUNT FOR POLICE KILLER

Along with the newsreader saying how a manhunt had already begun to find a boy who allegedly killed five police officers and taken hostage a young child. Members of the general public were advised not to apprehend the boy, as he was considered extremely dangerous.

"You okay, sweetie?" asked one of the assistants.

As Juliana wore an expression of absolute shock, the assistant continued. "Yeah, the young killers are the worst. Why don't you go sit down, and I'll arrange some more coffee for you?"

Juliana nodded and wandered in zombie-fashion towards the table, and sat down opposite Rocco.

"He's really done it now, hasn't he?" offered Rocco. Juliana said nothing in response, but dug her elbows into her lap, and propped her chin up with cupped hands. She closed her eyes so tightly, it hurt. After a few moments, she opened them again.

"This wouldn't have happened if we had stayed with him. We were stupid to go on the run. You don't have to do everything I say, Rocco."

"That's what our dear brother would say to me too," he smiled. "Could it be that both of you are wrong?"

"Don't get smart with me, Rocco. We have to figure out what to do."

"It's obvious. Embrace the life, as dear brother has."

"What do you think they will do when they catch him?"

"They did catch him. You just weren't paying attention, sis. Neither were they, it seems."

Juliana could understand why Marcus would kill, but not why he would kidnap someone. Whilst she was working this out in her head, the answer, one possible answer anyway, emerged.

"I am paying attention *now*," scolded Juliana. "He's taken someone because we ran out on him. He's going to make the child in the same mould as himself."

"You mean, make her a vampire."

"It's a girl?"

"That's what the news says."

Juliana wanted to look at the tv screen, but was simultaneously trying to make things look as normal as possible. At that same moment, the replacement drinks arrived.

"Here we go, you two," smiled the assistant. "Say, have you two ever been on tv before?"

"No," replied Juliana, "we have not."

"Well, I thought you had been in one of them commercials. A pair of angels is what you two are. I guess some people just win the gene pool lottery."

"Maybe. I suppose. Thanks for the coffees, and sorry about the mess."

"If you want anything else, just give us a shout."

Juliana nodded gratefully. She was also grateful that Rocco had kept quiet. She was even more grateful that no mention of herself and Rocco had been made so far.

"They've cut to another story," shrugged Rocco, and sat back in his seat.

"You're looking relaxed," said Juliana as she sipped her coffee.

"Well, we're free of him, see? It will only be a matter of time before they catch him. Again."

Juliana sighed heavily. She wanted to see the world in the same way that Rocco did, but it just wasn't that simple. If only Marcus had stopped at the kills. Why did he have to take someone away?

"We are not free of him, Rocco. He is controlling us, even now. He knew that the kills wouldn't be enough. Taking someone, he wants us to come after him. That's what he wants us to do."

"You think you can stop him? Good luck sis."

"We're going to stop him. Come on, get your things, Rocco. We will run no longer."

"Where are we going? You can't possibly know where he is."

"Oh but I do," Juliana said, punching her brother on the arm. "What would he said to you if you said something like that?"

"He'd say *I'm a vampire, brother.*"

"You just got your answer then."

Rocco understood. Juliana was taking them back to the cemetery.

Cemetery Gates

Juliana hadn't thought things through thoroughly, that much was certain. What was also certain; Marcus could be relied upon to be unpredictable. Fortunately, Juliana had one ace up her cotton jumper sleeve, and she doubted that even Marcus would be prepared for it.

Still, as they made the long journey back to the cemetery, Juliana knew he would be there. She just hoped the girl was safe. Once Marcus got something into his head, there was no way of turning it around. This time, however, Juliana believed things would be different. They just had to be.

Bringing Rocco along meant things could get complicated. She knew how manipulative Marcus was of his brother, and also that in a case of two-versus-one, she was likely to lose. Likely, but not for definite. Marcus did not hold all the cards; Juliana just needed to bet and win over him. Just this one time.

Looking around the cemetery, she could see a variety of headstones and gravestones. Some were quite simple, as in *Here Lies Kathleen Morris,* with a date added and nothing more.

Others were of children, who had their photo on the gravestone and had died from an age of only months to just a few years old. It was these younger ones that Juliana felt sorry for, but in another way, they would not live to see the kind of brutality that Marcus specialised in.

We are what we are, and we do what we do. That's what Marcus had told them whenever they deviated from the plan. His plan.

But Juliana did not agree with Marcus. In her view, *we are what we believe we are, and we become what we believe, and we live that life.* Because you can change elements of who you are, and you can decide to do something, or not. That's the real power humans hold. But so many humans believe who they are, and are shackled by something that may or may not be real, but their stupid, self-pitying beliefs make it so.

At least that is something I won't do, thought Juliana. *I will deal with what is real.*

The reality was that Marcus had to be stopped. Did she have what it took to truly kill her own brother?

***

"He could be behind any of them," said Rocco, gesturing to the stones.

Juliana shook her head. "No he won't, Rock."

"You know sis, sometimes *I* am right. He's waiting behind one of the small gravestones, waiting for just the right moment to jump out and scare the crap out of us."

Yes, sometimes Rocco could be right. But Marcus was hiding for two, unless he had hidden the girl somewhere. The fact that there were no police sirens closing in on them, meant that even they didn't have a clue where he was.

"It could be one of the larger gravestones, like that one with the angel over there," said Rocco brightly. "Let's hope he's hiding behind one of those."

"No," said Juliana truthfully. "Let's hope he's beneath one of those."

"Sis!" Rocco exclaimed. "You don't mean that!"

"Don't tell me you haven't thought the same thing as me, Rock."

With Rocco testing her with his bid to be heard, it could get all three of them killed. Marcus had already shown that his angelic face betrayed a fierce desire to kill, and she wasn't convinced that Rocco had been *made* in the same way that Marcus believed he was.

"Rocco, open your mouth."

"What?"

"Open. Wide. Now. I want to see what's in there."

"You *know* what's in there."

"Teeth. I know. But I'm looking for something else. Now show me."
"No."

"Pretend I'm Marcus, Rock. Play along."

"I'm not playing. Not with you."

Rocco's childish voice unsettled her a lot. Yes, they were young, but they were old too.

At least, Juliana felt like she had been around a long time. She could not remember a time before things had been, as they had always been.

We are what we are.

This line bothered Juliana immensely. *'What are we, then? We are just what we are at a point in time, right? So right now, that means we are trying to find this girl, and bring her home safely.'*

And we do what we do.

Well that was simple. Stop Marcus doing what ever he was doing.

"Rocco, you know what we are doing here, right? We have to stop Marcus. We have to return that girl safely."

For once, Rocco did not answer. Not straight away. Juliana was about to speak again, when finally, he responded.

"It's like you believe it's that simple. Stop Marcus, get the girl back, return her, no questions asked. Marcus has killed five cops, sis. Not to mention kidnapping a daughter of theirs. For our own part, we ran away from here like two kids who didn't know better. The police look dimly on that sort of thing, Jooly. Whatever we do, we're involved. We should be siding with Marcus, not against him."

Juliana took a step back, then two more, before there was a reasonable distance between herself and her brother.

"He got to you, didn't he? That's why you won't open your mouth."

"Oh sis, it's down to what you believe, isn't it?"

"Did he get to you or not?" Juliana clenched her fists. It wasn't beyond the realms of possibility for a girl to strike down a boy. She didn't want to hurt Rocco. She didn't want to hurt anybody. But right now, she found herself agreeing with Marcus about the whole *we are what we are* statement.

"You'll have to come closer to see, won't you?"

Juliana would not risk that. But something had changed since they had returned to the cemetery. Rocco had begun to talk in the authoritative tone that Marcus often used.

"You know where she is, don't you?"

"I might."

Now this was something Juliana could believe. Marcus and Rocco were very tight, much closer than Juliana was to either of them. It was clear that Marcus held Rocco under his control. Rocco had told her as much, even to the point of saying that he - Marcus, was frightened of his sister, because 'she's *different* to us, brother.'

Juliana would often sleep in a different part of the house, far away from her brothers. She would also sleep in a different way to her brothers. But to Juliana, it had always been this way. In her mind, it was her brothers who were the different ones.

Juliana finally decided to show them just how different they really were.

Where Angels are Made,
not Born

Rocco had done a runner. Juliana was okay with that. She knew the cemetery well, and it would only be a matter of time before she found Rocco and her darling brother Marcus.

The cemetery, strewn with Autumnal leaves tempered red, gold and brown, had an oddly calming effect on her, and as she walked slowly, but purposely, she wondered how long Marcus and Rocco could outrun her. After all, they had treated her pretty badly for someone who was different, which wasn't fair. It just wasn't fair.

Hadn't she treated them the same? She simply did not agree with Marcus' methods, and had told him so on many occasions. *'There has to be a new way of doing things,'* she had told them one time. Marcus had simply chosen to ignore what she had said.

'The old ways are dead,' she had told Marcus. Again, she had been ignored. Sometimes, you tell people something, they will listen to you. On other occasions, a simple tap on the shoulder, a word in their ear, will suffice.

For others, like Marcus, a mallet would have to be smashed squarely in his face. Then again, his preferred exit from this Earth would be via the vampire's bite.

Okay, so Rocco had made his choice and had sided with his brother. Juliana looked to the sky as she heard the screech of the bats. Three bats, flying in close formation to each other, and then….she realised they were not bats at all, much less the true thought in her head; that they were vampire bats.

Seagulls. Completely harmless.

"Rocco?" Juliana called out in various directions. "I'm not mad at you for running off. But it won't help you to side with Marcus just now."

Another screech in the sky. Clouds filled the expanse, covering the later afternoon hue in darkness. Juliana had to find the girl. She had to know she was safe. Marcus wouldn't understand. He constantly called his sister an *interfering meddler*, it has to be said that was one of his kinder names for her.

"Marcus! Let the girl go! The old ways are dead. Whatever you think you are, you're not. *Please*, let her go."

Juliana heard the sounds escape from her mouth. She did not like the sound of her voice. If the dead had ears to listen with, those that lay around her would say that she sounded like she was pleading. People like Juliana did not plead.

Juliana could hear a clinking sound. At first, it sounded like a glass bottle rolling down the tarmac, only for her to realise what it really was.

The cemetery was closing for the day, and the clinking sound was emitted from the gates being locked down.

"Noooo!" cried Juliana. She began to run in the direction of the gates, but this was a big cemetery, in which it didn't seem to have a centre of any kind. As the seconds passed, the darkness in the sky deepened. Soon, Juliana would only have the moonlight to show the way in front of her.

The cemetery staff could let her out, anyway. She wouldn't be locked inside. Oh, how she hated to be locked inside. Cemetery, wardrobe, coffin. It didn't matter; she disliked them all in equal measure.

The darkness closed in. Actually, Juliana responded much like a cat in these circumstances, with her eyesight getting keener and sharper, the more the light left the sky.

She came to a full stop, on the brow of a hill; with so many, *so many* graves surrounding her. But yes – she could make out the cemetery gates. There were three exits to this cemetery, and though it looked like it was closed already, a light was lit in the cemetery office.

On inspection, she could see clearly that the gates were locked. There was no way out. There had been some commotion in the office, so she ran towards it.

"Hello? *Hello?*"

Juliana did all she could to avoid her voice becoming a shrill.

The office, which had been lit up, exploded into darkness as one after one, the light bulbs shattered.

"Heeelllllllo?" The voice was now a shrill.

A light came on, with an object obscuring it. A human male, hanging from the wire, gargling his last. His feet tremored for a few moments, then stopped.

"Rocco? ROCCO! Tell me you didn't do that!" screamed Juliana. "Is Marcus with you? *Is he?*"

No answer.

"Answer me! Roc-"

Juliana turned around into something that felt like her face had bounced off a mountain. She felt fuzzy for a second, saw the room move with the now deceased man seeming to swing on the noose, as she fell to the floor.

                                   ***

Eventually, Juliana came to, and when she did, a familiar face was in front of her. But the face looked strange, like those animals that are stuffed to convince their owners that they are somehow still alive.

It was the girl, the daughter of that police officer. *Nina.* She didn't look quite right. Juliana squinted her eyes, and could see that Nina's head was intact. Marcus, who used a mallet to smash people's heads in, would have appeared to have left the girl alone.

Why did she look so strange then? The trauma of being kidnapped, she supposed.

The girl was trying to speak. Apart from her strange look, where for all the world she appeared to have been drugged, she seemed otherwise unharmed. Juliana craned her neck to hear what she was saying, but no words would come out. Eventually, the girl lifted her arm and pointed to something, or someone behind Juliana.

In the darkness, a simple word which filled her with terror.

"*Sister.*"

Definitely Marcus.

Juliana tried to get up, but Nina started to gesture wildly. Above Juliana, was some kind of spike, a sword of Damocles perhaps, but definitely something sharp. Her mind raced, and then the answer came to her.

It was a *stake*.

"Don't try to move, sis. It will only make things worse."

Marcus circled around his sister, before reaching above his head towards the stake, and pulled it down.

"It's for the best, Juliana."

"What? What are you on about?"

"You have to be stopped."

"Marcus? What's got into you?"

"Oh dear. She doesn't remember, brother. Stand, my sister. Slowly."

Juliana felt dizzy from the hit. Marcus had definitely whacked her with something. The side of Juliana's cheeks burned with the pain. It was like a hot iron had been placed on her face.

She could make out a shadow in the background, but it was clearly Rocco. The girl, Nina, remained rooted to the spot.

"Rocco? You're helping him? You're actually *helping* him?" That shrill again. Juliana really hated it when her voice did that. Why would Rocco side with Marcus, after all they had been through together? Marcus was the bad one.

"We got her away from you, but if this is what it takes, then go right ahead Juliana."

Maybe it was the haze of being hit by whatever it was, or the burning sensation on her cheek, but Juliana listened carefully to Marcus all the same.

"Go right ahead?"

"Yes. Kill her. After all, that's what you want, isn't it?" said Marcus. "Just let us live, sister. Let us go, unharmed. We don't want to die like those ones in the station. We won't tell anyone, we swear."

"Marcus, what are you on about?"

Juliana started to march towards Marcus, but he held the stake up.

"No sis. Not another step. Please don't."

Actually, there was a hint of fear in Marcus's voice. So Juliana complied, and stopped walking forward.

"So what now? You are still responsible for the murder of the Hills."

"It wasn't murder, Juliana."

Oh. She was not Jooly anymore.

"That sweet couple. I don't know how you can stand there and say that, Marcus."

"In the early days, yes, I'll admit, they were games. But they were dying, Juliana. I bet you didn't know that. Mr Hill asked me if I could make it look like an accident. I tried. I tried to involve Rocco. Made him think we were vampires. I really did think I was one. And then, there was you. How you scared us, sis. That's why I locked you in the wardrobe, though I knew you'd be mad once you got out."

"You're lying, Marcus."

"I am not. Mr Hill wanted out. He had stopped his meds. He didn't want to tell Mrs Hill."

"Still, how could you do it Marcus?"

To this question, he offered no direct answer, except to say, "Nellie Hall wanted it too. To go out with a bang on her birthday. We were helping her family, because you were threatening them."

Hazy details would come back to Juliana. Maybe she did threaten them. Maybe Marcus was right.

"Is your cheek still hurting?"

"Yes," Juliana replied, gritting her teeth. She could feel her fangs protruding. A memory of Mrs Hill saying, "Teeth! A pain coming, and a pain going."

Right on, lady, right on, thought Juliana.

"We're going to go now," said Marcus. "Don't follow us, sis, okay? The girl, she is a gift. Do her a favour, and finish her off. Don't....don't leave her like this."

Marcus backed off slowly, and then something fell from Juliana's face; a Holy Communion wafer that had been sticking to it.

It had burnt her skin.

She turned to look at little Nina, who looked so confused, so innocent, so angelic…much like themselves on occasion. Juliana's heart quickened, and soon, she had pulled little Nina towards her, and tasted her blood. Now, she realised everything. Now everything was clear. Now, Juliana realised why her brothers feared her.

She was a vampire. She had always been a vampire. Slowly, the memories came back, then hit her, wave after wave. Marcus had even tried to initiate Rocco into the game, using authentic fangs to sink into Mr and Mrs Hill. They had hoped that Juliana was not what they thought she was. They had hoped it was a game, and if it wasn't, that Juliana would be taken away and *corrected*, somehow.

That's why Marcus had insisted she join them on the hunt. She was the hunted, and she was the one they were trying to kill. She had simply avoided it, until now. The Holy Communion wafer was a distraction, whereas the stake could have killed her. The show of compassion from Marcus was not something she was going to share.

She had taken little Nina. She was setting up a new group of vampires.

And now, Nina, whose blood she had drank, would become one too.

Marcus had talked the talk, but had resisted for so long. Rocco, with nowhere else to go, was uncertain whose side he should take. No matter. Juliana watched as the boys began their run, and to be fair, had made good progress. But Juliana and her newest companion could move quick as light. They always could outrun the runners. Because fear makes you fall.

She grabbed Nina's hand, which by this time had turned cold.

"Don't be frightened," Juliana said, blood still dripping from her mouth. "This is just the beginning."

Juliana wiped the blood from her mouth, and walked towards the moonlight. Marcus and Rocco could run, but to vampires, such things didn't matter. They would be caught, and they would be *made*. A new dawn of vampires had arisen. For now, it was just Juliana and Nina, and as they morphed into vampire bats in search of their quarry, a third vampire bat joined them in the sky. One who had not died giving birth, after all.

In vampire bat form, Juliana signalled to her mother that Marcus and Rocco were just up ahead. "They need to embrace the life, as we do, Mother."

Juliana, her mother, and little Nina were true vampires. Marcus and Rocco had been merely playing at it.

No longer.

Soon, her brothers would join them.

The Blood and the Raven

Inspiration for
The Blood and the Raven

The first vampire story I ever read was Bram Stoker's Dracula. Like most children attending school, reading the classics was a major part of the school curriculum. But I actually enjoyed this book, I became more curious about the subject, and looked up other books in the genre.

Upon finding Anne Rice's Vampire Chronicles, I believed I had found the definitive vampire tale. Many years later, I still believe no-one is a higher authority on witches and vampires than Anne Rice.

Irish author Joseph Sheridan de Fanu's *Carmilla*, is another wonderful story that pre-dates Stoker's work – but is no less a classic in my view.

For a long time, I have wanted to tackle the vampire genre. In Autumn 2014, the first of seven novellas was released. Titled *Murderous Little Darlings: A Tale of Vampires: I*; I wanted to get back to what I thought vampires really were. In recent years, vampires have been repackaged as romantic figures, and this is not really how I see them.

Watching countless Hammer Horror movies as a child, the vampire, especially a female one, would appear as a seductress. But she was never meant to be the kind of entity that could be romanced. Vampires are killers. That's how Stoker wrote the character.

The 1992 movie of Stoker's classic was subtitled *Love Never Dies*. In the movie, the reincarnated Prince Vlad believes he has found his Elisabeta in the Victorian-day Mina Harker. If you've read the book, it is a stretch to believe it is a romance.

It works for Coppola's film, and whilst it was not scary, it had some good moments. But that was a long time ago. In this second Tale, I've attempted to make the subject matter more scary, more alarming. The vampires in the tale make no attempt at romance. They kill, and enjoy the very act. Such things should turn us off, and if I have done my job right, you will see vampires in the way that Stoker and Rice meant you to see them.

The Blood and the Raven: A Tale of Vampires II is the fifth fiction book I have had published.

One of the drinks mentioned in this book can actually be purchased in Birmingham. You'd have to go to The Wellington in the city centre to drink *Hung, Drawn and Portered*.

Five Candles

"**S**o she opens the door, and that's when he kills her."

"*And?*"

"What do you mean, *and*? She's dead. He's killed her. She's left the building. Pushing up the daisies. She's worm food. *She's dead.*"

"Sorry. I was just expecting something more scary."

Five teenagers sat in near darkness, two boys, three girls; candlelight shimmering on their faces. Each one hoped that they had a tale to tell, something that would make them fear going home alone. If it were memorable enough, a tale that would make them feel frightened even when it was daylight.

"Seth. It's your turn."

"No. It's late, you're all tired. I'm tired. And I'm not sure I want to be the last one to tell a story tonight."

"Oh come on, Seth. We all agreed to be here."

"Yes," he replied. "And we're here. So we can go home now."

"Are you *scared*, Seth?"

"No," he lied.

"Then come on. The story. Can't be any worse than anything else we've heard tonight."

Seth sighed heavily. After an age, he spoke. "I've heard the stories tonight, and frankly, they're boring. We've heard Dracula rip-offs. Two Twilight type tales. Jeez. There's even been one about robots. You really want to hear something scary? Well, I'll tell you. Because my story is based on true events-"

Raucous laughter erupted in the darkness.

"True events. That's what they always say, but it never is. Is this the infamous *Book and the Raven?*"

Although incorrectly stated, at the mere mention of the title, Seth stood up, and two of the candles the group were holding blew out.

"You see? You see what you're messing with?"

"That was just because you stood up too quickly. Now come on Seth, true events or not, we want to hear it. Three long years, it's been 'Oh, I'll tell you the story of the Book and the Raven.' Then you wimp out, and we never hear it."

"Fine. But I am not to blame if anything happens to you all, as a result of telling you this tale."

The group failed to contain their barely muffled laughs.

"So what's the title of your oh-so-scary story?"

"I have just one final disclaimer," said Seth. "Saying the name of this story is a little like saying Candyman five times. It's not to be messed with."

"Candyman Candyman Candyman Candyman Candy*muh*-" mocked Joel.

"I am not joking about this," said Seth, the pitch of his voice rising as he spoke. "Fine. Shut up and listen. *Shut. Up.* Yes. And you have got the title all wrong. The actual name of the story is-"

"Hang on," said Daisy. "I'm pretty shook up as it is. And it will be long after midnight when Seth finishes his story, right? I am just raising my objections. If this story is anything like what Seth is saying, we should vote."

"Voting?" sneered Joel. "It's just a stupid story."

"Of the five of us, two candles have blown out," said Gretchen. "Yours, Joel, and yours too, Anna. You're mocking Seth's story. That's why, every year, when we all meet up, he refuses to tell it. I know why he refuses; it's with good reason too."

"Because.....he's full of it," exclaimed Joel. "Seth is alive, which puts his story all out of whack. Why would he be left alive, if it were true? He'd be dead too."

"Unless he actually *killed* those he told the story to," laughed Anna. "Seth, I always thought you did have a dark side about you."

"All the same," added Daisy, "I don't think we should mock anyone. Especially here, in this place. It's eerie. Far too quiet. I

don't like it. But we agreed to be here because this is the last time
we'll all be together. Seth is right. We agreed to come here, and we
did. Let's quit while we're ahead."

"You're being far too dramatic," mocked Anna.

"We are leaving school," said Daisy. "It's a special time. It won't
happen again. Each moment of our lives that pass, they will never
come again."

"That's pretty deep, my philosophical friend," said Joel. "But I just
want to hear about the stupid virgin who gets ravaged by her
boyfriend, who – oops – turns out to be a vampire. Then he
sacrifices her to Satan. The end. No voting. Just story telling. Make
it a scary one. Now hurry up Seth, I am freezing out here."

Seth had remained quiet. He wanted to get the details of the story
absolutely right, with nothing left out. But where to start? Seth
composed himself and began to tell the story. When he had
finished; *if* he could finish – then maybe the curse would be lifted.
Five candles had been lit, but already two were extinguished. Seth
would have to hurry.

The Blood and the Raven

The rain hammered down, making a mockery of the road in front of the man and the woman. They made their way towards shelter, trying to stay inside the carriage as it moved at a speed they were unaccustomed to. The horseman was silent.

"Say, would you slow down a little?" asked the man.

The horseman did not reply.

"Did you hear what I said?"

Same response.

"Hmmph!" the man grunted as he sat back in his seat, and battled to keep the window shut. "Once they are paid, you don't hear from them again."

"Dear," said the woman gently, but in a tone that could not hide that she had seen this behaviour from her husband in the past, "the most important thing is that we arrive safely."

"At this rate, we will be left for dead in a ditch," he replied. "I say! Slow down!"

The horseman finally responded to the man's request.

"There," said the man. "Working class type. Should be used to commands from his masters. Seems he forgot his manners."

"*Shh,*" his wife urged. "He might have heard you."

"I should jolly well hope so."

Both the man and his wife were nearly thrown forward by the force of the carriage coming to an abrupt halt. The man shouted at the horseman, inquiring in none too discreet a fashion, as to *what the hell do you think you're doing?*

The horseman said nothing, but pointed to a light in the distance.

"You're ordering us off? You're actually doing that? I have a lady here, don't you know? You uneducated brutish oik! How dare you!"

"You and your lady will be welcome at The Raven," stated the brutish oik.

"Excuse me?"

"The Raven. Or to give you its full title, *The Inn of the Blood and the Raven.*"

"What kind of a name is that for a place of shelter?"

"I wouldn't know about such things, being uneducated as I am."

With that, the horseman whipped his horses into a gallop. The man and his wife had little choice but to make their way to the strangely named inn.

"Your cousin mentioned nothing of this place," his wife offered. "Maybe the horseman has gotten us lost."

"Or maybe he got us to exactly where he meant to take us," said the man ruefully. "No matter. Public houses often have unusual names. This could be one of those quirky ones. Don't let it unsettle you, my dear."

"I'm fine," she replied. "In fact, it's all rather interesting. In London, all the public houses have stock names; being called The Queens Head, or the Kings Head, or something like that."

"Well this is the Midlands, dear. I just want to be in, then out. There's not one reason to stay in this godforsaken place any longer than we need to."

"What exactly do you have against the Midland folk, dear?" she asked.

He declined to answer at that particular moment in time, but ushered her through the door. The pub sign above showed the picture of a raven. No mention or illustration of blood. Just a simple looking raven.

No doubt that raven was drawn - poorly drawn, by a simple minded Midlander, thought the man.

Inside the tavern, the scene looked normal, and was at odds with the tumultuous rain that hammered down on the outside.

The stools and tables of exquisite Victorian design, were packed with well-dressed people in the main. There were a few people who could have been considered of being the *uneducated variety* that the man hated to be in the same room with. However, outside, there remained few options, so he elected to stay indoors.

He motioned to his wife, who sat down by the only available corner in the public house. The rain splattered by the window, which didn't unnerve her. Actually, it reassured her – she was glad to be in from the cold, wet conditions.

Her husband was ordering some drinks at the bar. A sherry wine for his wife, an ale for himself.

His wife noticed something as the rain relentlessly pounded at the window. The rain was blood coloured. She removed her glasses, squinted her eyes, then looked again. No. She had been mistaken. Simple, pure rain water.

As well as the incessant pounding of the rain, she was sure she could hear something else. A fluttering of something - something she could not determine at that time, what it was.

"Ah, the Raven has marked you, I see," said a man.

"I do not know you, sir," replied the woman. "It is inappropriate for you to address a lady so."

"That may be the case in London," said the man. "But you are far from London. I just noticed droplets of blood on you. The Raven must have made another kill."

"Excuse me?"

"The Raven," replied the man. "We used to have a huge population of pigeons, and people for that matter. This pub was so named because of the beast."

"A beast? It's a simple bird, surely?"

"Ah, perhaps so in London. But here, the Raven has been seen in different forms. It-"

"Mr O'Mahoney, I like to make the guests welcome here. No scare stories please."

A lady had appeared from behind the bar. She was elegantly dressed, and the woman observed that her style would not have been out of place in London's most fashionable balls. The lady was tall, perhaps six feet tall, dark, raven like hair, coifed into a bun, with ringlets hanging either side of her prominent cheekbones.

She wore a dress the very colour of midnight, a square cut on the chest line, with the most delicate and elegant beading adorning the edge of the dress. It was an empire style; and there was no denying it was worn to make an impression.

"My name is Mariana Dreymuir, and I am the owner of this little establishment. Welcome to our pub. Make yourself at home at The Raven."

Her accent did not sound like someone local to the Midlands, not even local to England. She extended a gloved hand to the woman, and she observed that through her slim fingers, a vice-like grip kept a hold of her. Mariana looked into the woman's eyes, and smiled.

Their gaze was broken by the man at the bar, who had lost any sense of patience he might have had.

"I want to order drinks, if you have finished interrupting my wife's evening," he said curtly.

His wife looked on in horror at him. "Don't be so rude, dear. This is -"

She paused, and looked sheepishly around her, before returning her gaze towards the lady. "I'm so sorry, I forgot your name."

"Mariana." She smiled the kind of smile that could melt the coldest of souls. That accent? Where was it from? The woman could not place it.

"I am so sorry," she said to the man. "Tonight is our busiest night, and of course, our population has increased by two this evening."

Nervous sniggers filled the room. Mariana continued to put the man at ease, not shaking his hand, but lightly touching his arm. She was taller than him by a good four inches. The man, also lost in her gaze, tempered his annoyance somewhat, almost to the point that he was embarrassed by his actions.

"It-it-it's me who should apologise," he stammered, but fought to control it. "My wife and I have travelled from London, the weather was most terrible, and we happened upon your wonderful establishment."

"And you are most welcome," said Mariana. "Please be seated. Enhance our evening with your presence!"

She clapped her hands abruptly, like one of those Spanish flamenco dancers.

"Juliana! Come down here now! We have *new* guests!"

"Aye, and new blood too!" said a voice. More sniggering from amongst the group. The man finally took his place next to his wife, and looked around to see who was sniggering. His wife noticed his discomfort, patted his arm gently, and he slunk back into the seat, trying not to be noticed. He also tried not to look back at the beautiful landlady, Mariana.

He had been married to his young wife for three years. She was eighteen at the time, whilst he was forty-four. Now she was twenty-one, the difference didn't seem so bad. Plus, with her headscarf and glasses, she looked older than she was. He had encouraged her use of the word 'dear' to further engender this view.

Mariana. She invaded his thoughts. She looked about his age – forty-seven, but did she look good for her age. No real visible signs of wrinkles, no greying hair, piercing brown eyes. And then, there was that dress, that clung effortlessly around her curves. Her being tall just accentuated the whole, mesmerising vision. She had an essence, a strange, alluring scent coming from her too.

Upstairs, Juliana stirred slowly from her slumber. Something had tried to wake her before her mother called for her to work at the bar. The raven, which perched on her window sill, flapped its wings, once, twice, three times, before swooping downward, out of view, and killing something. A bird. A cat. *A human*.

Then, it would resume its place on the window sill. No amount of 'shoo-ing' would remove it. Juliana didn't care for the bird at all. But it tried so hard to get into her favour, tap-tapping on the window with its beak.

Some nights, Juliana would wake with a start, as the raven would have something in its mouth. The neck of a small bird, which it would crush with its powerful hooked beak. The fur and bloody tissue of some animal it had killed. Tonight, it was a finger. A human finger.

Juliana sprung from her bed and hurriedly closed the curtains.

"Go away, wretched bird!"

The raven disgusted her. She had even asked her mother to change the name of the pub, which had been met with girlish sniggering. From a woman of her years, that was quite something. Then again, her mother often reminded Juliana, who could pass for a young woman of eighteen summers, not to forget her inner child.

She had also told Juliana, in no uncertain terms, to *leave the raven alone*.

She threw a simple tunic over her dress, and ran downstairs.

"Juliana," said her mother warmly, and embraced her. "We have new guests. Please tend to them. An ale for the gentleman, and a sherry for his lovely young wife."

"But I didn't say what drinks I wanted," offered the man.

"Oh, you look like an ale man," smiled Mariana. "As for your wife, she looks too young for gin. But we can get you whatever you would like."

"How about *Hung, Drawn and Portered?*" shouted a voice amongst the crowd.

"Yeah, and a *Raven's Blood* for the lady!" shouted another. The sniggers had become laughter, uncomfortable to the man, but Mariana continued her smile as if she had not heard a thing.

"An ale," ordered Mariana. "Gorgon's Blood, and a Pitcher's sherry for the lady. Make sure it is a lady's glass."

"Yes ma'am," replied Juliana courteously.

With the drinks warming their throats and bellies, the couple began to relax. "I say," said the man, "this is excellent – a really excellent brew. Where do you brew this? I should like to visit there one day."

"Derbyshire," replied Mariana, who worked other tables in the pub, but returned on frequent occasions to their table. "It is about an hour and a half from here, as the crow flies."

"Even quicker if it is the raven doing the flying," laughed a voice.

The man looked around to see who was laughing, but it was so hard to tell. Every one of the punters appeared to be looking the other way. It was most disconcerting to the man, but he decided to think no more of it.

Juliana brought the drinks over. The woman observed her on approach, and was almost transfixed by the girl's appearance, who perhaps was a similar age to herself.

Juliana placed the drinks on the table, and to the woman's surprise, sat next to her. "I hope you're enjoying your stay. You are strangers to this town. You would do well to stay the night, now the hour is late."

The woman thought Juliana spoke very eloquently for someone of her years; the thought that Juliana was like an old woman in a young girl's body did cross her mind.

"We haven't decided yet," replied the woman. She gave her husband a nudge, whose gaze was being held by Mariana, who had returned to the bar. "Have we, dear?"

"No," he said, rather absent-mindedly. Turning to Juliana, he ventured the question that was in his mind. "Say, young lady. There is a lot of chittering about *the raven* and so on. Do the locals want to upset us for some reason?"

His wife thought it rather forward of him to ask. At the same time, she believed it to be a fair enough question. Juliana leaned forward, as if she was going to answer, then sat back again. She placed a hand underneath her chin, continuing to gaze at the woman.

"*Chittering?*" replied Juliana, after what seemed like an age. "Cats chitter, but not people, and certainly not ravens!"

"I meant no disrespect," said the man. "We are from London, you know."

His wife dropped her head forward in disbelief. As if this Juliana would not know that!

"Many of the punters drink more than they should, and so, speak more than they should," offered Juliana simply. "They mean no disrespect either. Just men, being men. Please, take your time with your drinks. I will bring you more shortly. Then I will show you to your rooms."

"Excuse me? *Rooms*?" exclaimed the man. "We are married. We require one room only."

"Your ways, those of London, are perhaps not our ways," said Juliana cryptically. "Here, a lady stays with her maid. She will not lie with any man, not even her husband."

"Preposterous!" The man's voice raised to a shout. "Dear, we are *leaving*."

The woman said she did not feel well, but her husband was insistent. He hurried his wife into her coat, and pushed her towards the door. She claimed that she could see dots in front of her eyes. As she lapsed into a standing faint, she claimed the dots were in fact *eyes*. Black eyes.

"The eyes of the raven," she murmured.

Juliana said no more, but returned to behind the bar, with the *lady's glass* in her hand. "Sorry, mother. They left, despite my best intentions."

Mariana propped her daughter's head up by placing her fingers under her chin. "They have left. For now."

Outside, the rain which had showed no sign of stopping, had worsened since the man and his wife had been inside the Blood and the Raven.

"Damned place," the man said, covering his head from the rain as much as he could, Then, his expensive hat blew away as a strong gust of wind rose out of nowhere. He found he could not cradle his wife and keep his head protected at the same time.

He shouted out in the darkness for a carriage. The wind howled, the rain hammered, the icy night bit, and bit hard. At least the cold kept his wife from collapsing.

To his amazement, a four-horse carriage appeared, led by a figure in black.

"Take us to…..Derbyshire," said the man, "and away from this cursed place!"

The figure said nothing, and the man ushered his wife into the carriage. As soon as they were inside, the horses broke into a gallop uncomfortable for the man, and he was about to complain about that to his wife, when she spoke ahead of him.

"Juliana had offered us rooms! Why didn't you take her up on the offer?"

"Hmmph!" said the man irritably. "Rooms. Could have been just one room. That creepy girl and her mother just wanted to make money out of us. And the way she was looking at you. Most improper. This sort of thing might be okay for the Midlanders, but not us."

"What irritates you more, *dear* – the fact she wanted us in separate rooms, or that Juliana was looking at me?"

"Stop such infantile talk. I cannot believe we are having this conversation."

"What is infantile, *dear*, is travelling on such a night when the road ahead is closed."

"What?"

"There's no way through. We will have to turn back. You'll see. The horseman will turn around in a moment."

The man ignored his wife. The drink must have been stronger than both of them could manage. His wife was rambling, thinking that someone else was looking at her with desire, least of all – another woman.

The horses whinnied and slowed to a trot, and without saying anything, the horseman about-turned the carriage. The man shouted out to him to continue ahead, but the horseman shook his head, and pointed towards the road ahead, which looked like it had been torn apart. By what, or by whom, it was not known.

All that was known, was that there was no way to traverse the gap in the road.

There was no escape from Birmingham, and no way to go to Derbyshire. With no other options available to them, they headed back to the Blood and the Raven.

Night Terrors

Seth's continuance of the tale was broken by Daisy, who shrieked as the light on her candle flickered, almost put-putting out as she spoke.

"Seth, come on now. There would be other routes out of Birmingham, not just one way."

She hugged herself. "God, it's cold. How much more of the story, Seth?"

"When I'm done, I'm done," replied Seth. "When any of you interrupt me, it slows the tale up, and breaks my concentration. May I remind you that two candles have already blown out? Why would you want to mess with that, Daisy?"

"I'm not messing with anything," answered Daisy, in far more sharp a tone than she meant to. "I'm just cold."

"Tell the truth, Daise," smirked Joel, whose candle had already burned out, and refused to be lit again. "You're scared. Maybe it's the silent horseman. Maybe it's the raven. Maybe you're freaked out about what Seth said, that when the tale is told, people begin to die."

"Maybe I am just wanting Seth to finish, so we can be out of this Godforsaken place, and I don't have to listen to you anymore," said Daisy stiffly, whilst at the same time acknowledging to herself that

Joel's barbs were hitting close to the bone, and held more truth than she would like to admit.

"*Stay lit, stay lit,*" she whispered to the candle, which barely held its flame.

"You'll be going down with Joel and me," laughed Anna. "Our candles burned out long ago."

"Just quit that, will you?" snapped Daisy. "Seth? I hope you are just pulling our legs about the whole *people die once they hear this story*, thing."

Seth did not reply directly to Daisy's question, electing instead to ask one of his own.

"May I continue? The night is no longer young, and the candles are burning down."

His words did not sound like those of a modern teenager. This was old-world speak, and it made Daisy even more uncomfortable.

"Okay Seth," said Daisy, with barely disguised irritability in her voice. "Just crack on."

Gretchen nodded in agreement, whilst Joel and Anna continued to make ghoul and ghost sounds. Seth gave them a disparaging look, and decided to carry on. He had to finish the tale, because he needed to lift the curse, and selfishly, that was all that mattered to him.

***

The horse carriage containing the man and his young wife trotted back slowly to the Inn of the Blood and the Raven. The horses seemed reluctant, and trudged their hooves through sodden clay, that barely hung well enough together to qualify as a road.

The couple travelled on in silence. There was an uneasy feeling about returning to the Inn, though the woman was secretly intrigued to be seeing the young Juliana again. For the man's part, his thoughts were all about the voluptuous Mariana.

On arrival at the Inn, the couple's excitement dimmed as the place appeared to be in complete darkness. Could it really have emptied that quickly? The man checked his watch, and he could scarcely believe his eyes. Three hours had passed, and the hands were striking three in the morning.

He made huge exclamations to his wife; in the vein of *how is this possible*, and *what kind of place is this?*

She merely shrugged, and suggested that they hope someone will answer them at the Inn. How she really hoped to see Juliana again. This strange girl had really enchanted her. *Mesmerised* her. Yes, mesmerised. That was a much better word to describe her feelings towards this young woman. She just had to see her again. Why this was, she had no idea. There was just something unearthly about the girl. In her short life, she had never encountered anyone like this before.

The couple stood outside the main door. A bird clung to the pub sign, which creaked above them.

"A blackbird," said the man. "One which has found the wrong sign to cling to. There's no need to be nervous, my dear."

"I'm....not nervous," replied his wife. *Not at all.* That said, she was not convinced the avian was a blackbird, it seemed much too large for that. The bird suddenly squawked, and the woman could have sworn that the bolts on the door had slid to an unlocked position.

There was no need to bang the door down, as it simply swung open.

"How strange," said the man. "Well, at least we can find shelter for the night."

But the Inn was in darkness, and their carriage left as soon as they had vacated it.

They walked along the corridor, and their eyes strained to see what lay ahead.

The man shouted out, but no-one replied. Finally, after looking in each room, one door, which appeared to lead towards downstairs, could not be opened. A cold, dank air emitted from the keyhole slot. *And something else*, thought the man.

"It smells like death down there," said the man. "I don't like this at all."

Whatever the man had inhaled, in the cold night air the vapour passed from his mouth and into his wife.

What happened to them next would change their lives forever.

***

"Perhaps we should just look elsewhere for shelter," said his wife wearily. "It's late, or early, depending on your disposition. I for one, require rest. Make a decision, will you?"

She had not meant to sound so impertinent, but this had already been such a strange night; and where was Juliana anyway? The woman could not explain why, but she was anxious to see her again.

Whilst she ran this thought through her head, the previously locked door opened, and something pulled the man inside, before the door slammed shut again. The woman caught a gust of the dead air, which first filled her nostrils and then; her stomach, with disgust. She retched a little before managing to compose herself.

"Dear? Where are you? Where did you go?"

She banged on the door, but its metal was damaged by the rust of many years. Even so, it had opened and shut without any apparent difficulty. Her husband had not disappeared, but was merely on the other side. That was her reasoning, and she was sticking by it.

Her worry turned to joy as she felt the presence of someone. She could not see who it was, but she could *feel* her. Yes, definitely Juliana.

She seemed to have materialised out of nowhere. But the woman forgot all about that. To her, Juliana was magical. *Magical.*

"You need rest," said Juliana simply. "Come. I will show you to your room."

The woman followed Juliana. Neither of them mentioned the missing man. The Inn, deceptively small on the outside, was massive on the inside. Juliana never looked back towards to the woman to see if she was still following her. She walked – no, *glided* ahead of the woman, a half-smile on her face.

Her skin was pearl white, but with the pub's sepia lighting, she looked all-aglow.

However, only small candle-light provided any illumination to the dark surroundings. But as the woman was in the company of Juliana, she noticed only her; not any of the surroundings. Even though they seemed to be walking for a very long time, and covered some distance, they seemed no closer to a bedroom.

Finally, Juliana stopped moving. They had been going north for quite while, then perhaps a slight deviation to the western point of the building. Juliana produced a key, a large, oversized one that looked like it belonged to the Queen herself. A key that surely had no place in opening doors, but should have been carried on a velvet cushion, as was the tradition in the palace of Westminster.

She placed it in the lock, and before the woman's eyes, the key appeared to turn itself, before disappearing into the lock, far from view. A satisfying click was heard, and the door opened slowly.

"You may go in now. You will have an excellent sleep, I'm sure. I will check on you later."

The woman said nothing. For a reason that escaped her entirely, she found herself in awe of the beguiling, resplendent Juliana.

The room was elegant, and full of wondrous detail. A gold wallpaper with an embossed red crest. Several paintings, most of them portraits. One of them was of Juliana. Two others were of boys, one with a cheeky impish grin. The other had an innocent look about him, but was looking over his shoulder, as if he was being chased by someone or something. Chased, or *hunted*.

In hotel rooms, a bible was often found in one of the drawers on the dresser. In this room, the woman checked, but there was no Holy Bible to be found. There was sometimes a crucifix on the wall. Not so here. In fact, there were no religious items of any kind to be found.

From her earliest recollection, the woman had bore an aversion to jewellery. Her husband had purchased a watch for her, only for it to stop functioning within a day of her wearing it on her slender wrist. She wore only a simple necklace with a pendant on it.

The room also felt unusually cold. The main public house seemed to be warm, she recalled. Still, the bed had a generous amount of blankets, plump pillows, and a duvet full to bursting with duck feathers.

Juliana had said so, hadn't she?

You'll have an excellent sleep, I'm sure.

What in the world did she mean by that?

The woman slipped into the bed, and she could soon understand. This bed, was without, the most comfortable bed she had ever slept in. The mercury may have dropped in the room, but the woman hardly noticed.

Her eyes flickered open, then shut, in the kind of uncomfortable condition that insomniacs find themselves.

I'll check on you later.

There was no need to do that, surely? It was after three a.m. There was no need to check on anything. Except to know where her husband was.

Whilst she was pondering that mystery, she fell into the deepest sleep.

In the dream, she could see the gates leading towards her driveway, which was about a half mile long in itself. Whilst her husband worked in London, they lived in Ascot. But she accompanied him on the journey on many occasions, meeting friends in the city to while away their time.

The pleasant homely image passed into something else. She could feel something on her, holding her down. A woman, with long nails, and a unique perfume about her. Her hair caressed the woman's cheeks, and she could see something around her neck.

A cross.

No. It had been a cross at one time, but it had burned itself onto the woman, branding her forever. This woman was known to her.

Juliana.

I'll check on you later.

Was she checking on her *now*? In her dream-like state?

The woman woke from her tormented sleep to find the vampire biting deep into her neck. Her strength was incredible; her vice-like grip inescapable.

She tried to speak, move, react, do something or *anything;* but there was no way she could overpower this…whatever this was.

The woman was dizzy, for she realised that she was not merely being bitten, on her neck, no less, she was being *drained*. Her fingers trembled, her arms contorted, her back stiffened as the vampire pulled her closer and bit harder and deeper.

Finally, she pulled away, blood on her mouth, and spoke to the woman, trying to allay her fears.

"You see your blood on my lips. The blood is the essence of life. Were it to leave your body, you face death. Is this what you want? Or do you still desire that which you call a life, with that man?"

"I-I don't know," said the woman, who appeared to be in a trance-like state. "I don't know. It….it hurts when you….what did you do?"

The woman felt around her neck and her fingers could soon trace the puncture wounds that felt icy to the touch. She regarded Juliana, who was knelt on the bed in front of her. She wore a pale yellow nightdress that barely encased her considerable cleavage. She would have appeared beautiful, like an angel from heaven, but for the blood on her mouth, which she made no attempt to remove. Her skin looked almost ivory in colour. It was not a normal pallor.

Then, all these strange questions. The ones she was asked would provide no answers of any comfort. The ones she was asked would only serve to heighten her sense of terror.

Juliana's allure and playfulness was lost in that moment. "You saw it in your dreams, didn't you?"

The woman could barely nod a yes, but Juliana took it as such.

"The raven."

"Yes," she replied, an unsteadiness in her voice. "I have seen it, even before I came to this place. Wings beating at my window. Black feathers strewn over my bed, and my husband's throat – "

She paused, as if each word was like walking barefoot on hot coals.

"Go on," Juliana replied, but it seemed more like an order to continue than a request. "What was the raven doing?"

"It appeared for all the world to be feeding on my husband's flesh. Goring his neck and chest. It doesn't bear thinking about."

"You know why, don't you?"

"I don't wish to say. It is a matter between a man and his wife."

The woman slumped back on the bed, blood oozing from her neck. Juliana moved quick-as-lightning to her side, grabbed her wrist with one hand, and touched her forehead with the other.

"This is a matter between you and your *life*. Do you not you owe it better than this? If you must be mute, then I'll tell you what I know. Three years long and yet, your marriage has not been consummated. Your husband looks old enough to be your father and….he is impotent. At least, that is what he told you, is it not? The truth now!"

The woman was weary from the night's events. But her eyes widened at Juliana's perceptiveness.

"He is so, but he is a good man. He looks after me."

"Just like he's looking after you right now?"

There was a creeping sense of menace in the vampire's voice.

"Shall I tell you where he is at this moment? Or perhaps you should see, before death takes you."

The woman began to walk towards Juliana, as if to say something. Her legs brushed awkwardly by the bed, and she slowed to a crawl.

"I feel…I feel unwell. I must lie down."

"You are beginning to feel anew. Your body is playing its part. Don't be frightened."

The woman maintained her unsteady stance, and wavered as if intoxicated.

"I don't wish to take your life. I'm simply offering you a new one. You can feed, and feast, on a new man every night. Or a woman. I would stay away from animals though if I were you."

"You're a monster!"

"Both you and your husband are the monstrosities, trying to convince those around you of the charade you call a marriage. Fraudsters, the pair of you!"

The woman found she could no longer stand, and collapsed on the bed. "I'm not a fraud."

"Oh really?" asked Juliana whimsically. "Then it must be your husband who is the fraud, pleasuring my mother as he is now, instead of you."

The woman appeared to be losing consciousness. Juliana leaned over her and breathed on her neck. "Not yet. You cannot go just yet. Besides, I have not taken enough blood for you to die. Should you want to die, I can do that."

"You talk as if I have options."

"Of course you do. You can be like me. You'll see the world through new eyes. You will see things differently, that is for certain. Come with me now."

The woman protested, saying she could barely stand. Juliana dragged her onto her feet, and ushered her out of the room, and into the narrow hallway. In a room two doors down, the woman could hear some commotion. A man, and a woman engaged in….the woman could barely comprehend it.

"No!" she cried. "No! What's he doing?"

"Humans do make the most amazingly pointless statements," said Juliana, allowing herself a wry smile. "Of course you know what he's doing. You bored him. Were too sedate. I bet he would be interested in you now, though."

The woman slid down the wall, and convulsed slightly.

"Wh-what is happening to me?"

"You're dying. So is your husband. At least the pretence of your marriage ends tonight."

"I don't want to die. I don't deserve to die."

"So ask me to save you from this death, and I will."

The woman nodded. It was not clear if she understood the gravity of her decision. Juliana lifted her into her arms and bit deep, much deeper this time. The woman's body shook violently, before becoming still. Juliana was practised at this, and it was getting easier each time. The woman limply surrendered to the floor.

Her eyes flickered as the life was taken from her. Juliana seemed to be standing at one point. At other moments, she appeared to be hovering above her.

The woman, too weak to move, became aware of the reason Juliana had moved herself. A sound of wings beating smattered against the door, and a liquid formed around the woman's body. Blood. The blood of the man she had married.

She was now fully aware.

"The Raven! Oh my! It's in there. It's killing him!"

She stood up, and went to wrench the door open, and whilst she partially managed it, Juliana held her back.

Inside, the man was on his back, his legs and feet were facing the headstand, and his head nearest the doorway. His arms were placed in an outward direction, and he resembled a cross. The kind of cross that would be used at a black mass.

As the woman surveyed the horror, she observed his neck had been gored away by someone or more accurately, some *thing*. No human could have possibly done that.

His eyes had been ripped from their sockets, leaving gaping, bloody holes. His chest was strewn with black feathers.

As the woman ran to him, she could feel something behind her. Not Juliana. A shadow lay in the corner of the room. A human, but in the guise of a bird. The figure was covered in black feathers. The face appeared to be human, yet it was darkened in the shade of the bird. A raven. The fingernails bent in menacingly, and she had seen that shape before. On the bird's beak, no less.

"I-I must get back to London," breathed the woman hoarsely. "What in God's name is going on here?"

"Two things about *here*," said the Raven-Woman. "There is no God here, and there is no leaving here."

The Raven-Woman morphed into bird form and flew out of the window, only to perch on the sign, blood pouring down it from her claws. The Raven let out just the one squawk, and the locals knew what it meant.

"Just the one kill tonight then," one of them said, somewhere in the darkness.

"For now," thought the Raven to itself.

A New Way of Living

Juliana ushered the woman in a room that lay far beyond the hall, deep within the bowels of the Inn. If it were possible, it was even darker in this area, and they would not have been able to see at all, if only for oil lamps that lit the way ahead, though these were sparse in their number.

The woman did not say much, though murmured that she needed to lie down. Juliana ignored her words, merely directing her ahead, gesturing to her that they did not have much farther to go.

The woman, still new to this existence, felt the change in the air. No warmth emanated in this area, and surely that was the stench of death in the air? Was it her own body? She could not tell.

"I need to rest!" It sounded more like an order than a request, and it compelled Juliana to turn around and look at the woman, who looked terrified at what had become of her.

"Well then," replied Juliana cheerfully, "We have come to the right place! Look! This is for you!"

In the darkness, the woman could make out a shape, oblong, she thought at first, though it appeared to be wider at the top end.

"A coffin!"

Juliana ignored the obvious shock in her voice, and continued in a cheery manner.

"You're welcome. Yes, and all for you, too. I had to share with my brothers for a while. When we were smaller. But you're already an adult. Most people are already dead when they are put in one of these. How lucky you are to see this day! Anyway, jump in! Sweet dreams."

Juliana walked some twenty feet towards her own coffin, and lifted the lid, only to be stopped by the woman screaming. Juliana turned around, exasperated.

"What is it *now*?"

"You cannot seriously expect me to get into this…this…thing?"

"What else do you expect to do? To lie down, as a human does, that is not for us. For *you*. Anymore."

"I'm dead? I'm really dead?!"

"Yes, of course you are. You can see me, can't you?"

"Yes. But I don't care for stupid questions." She replied as if it was the most obvious statement in the world, disliking Juliana's ridiculing of her immensely.

"Well done. You are dead," replied Juliana. "I took the liberty of removing the soil from the hooves of the horses that brought you here. The soil of your home county, no less. You will feel at home here, just take the time to get used to this new existence, and I will show you some more tomorrow."

The woman turned and ran in the opposite direction, only for Juliana to appear right in front of her.

"How-how did you do that?"

"I thought you didn't care for stupid questions. Now get in your coffin!"

Juliana gave the woman the lightest touch on her arm, only to see her fly backwards towards the open coffin. As quick as thought, Juliana slammed the coffin lid down, the density of the casket unable to stifle the woman's screams.

"Scream all you like," said Juliana. "But I want you to calm it down in a bit. I need my rest too."

Juliana glided over to her own coffin, and without making any noise at all, entered the coffin and shut the lid.

She was thankful that she could not recall when she had been made a vampire. She could not imagine it being pleasant. Not pleasant at all.

The bangs on the lid subsided, and finally, the screams fell silent.

"It'll all make sense in the morning," murmured Juliana.

***

Inside the coffin, the woman was quiet, but not asleep.

"It's a dream. A nightmare. Obviously. I'll wake from this, and I'll be with my dear husband, and of course it's not real. I would be terrified if this was really a coffin. I can breathe, so it's not a real coffin. None of this is happening."

She replayed these thoughts over and over again, until sleep, the scent of black earth, and the rich mahogany wood took her.

***

Juliana, meanwhile, was busy in the town. She visited a number of shops, purchasing an array of meat, vegetables and fruit. Not for herself of course, but the façade had to be kept up. Besides, none of it would go to waste, as the new addition would not have enough strength yet to stand as a vampire on her own.

"Here, Miss," said one of the men, "don't you be venturing up the road, there. It's been damaged by something not of God's earth. "None of us will be able to pass until they've fixed it."

"Oh, I'm sure someone will find a way if they need to."

"She knows about the road, you old coot," said another man. "She works at The Raven!"

"Is that true, Miss? You work at that ungodly place?"

"What's ungodly about it?" smiled Juliana. "It is but a mere pub, where gentlemen and ladies can relax after a hard day's work. Or a leisurely one, for that matter."

"Miss, leave that accursed place, and let me take you to the priest. He is a man of God."

"I'm sure that's what he told you. Though that sort of thing didn't go down too well two thousand years ago, did it? Give or take a century."

The man pulled out a crucifix and held it in front of Juliana. He called her a blasphemer, and she grabbed his arm, twisting it until it broke. She stamped her foot on the crucifix, and while she winced at the contact, it disintegrated on impact.

The man cradled his broken arm.

"You witch! Servant of Satan!"

"What happened to *Miss*?"

She turned to the other man. "I can let you two off with a warning. But if you interfere with me again, it will be the last thing you'll ever do on this Earth. Tell your priest *that*!"

"He just wanted to help you," offered the other man. "I know what pains you. I know the one who made you as you are. If you would just take me to her, I can set you free."

"You think there is one above *me*?" snapped Juliana. "That's the problem with you religious types. You believe in some kind of hierarchy. You want to take us down, then come tonight to The Raven, and bring your priest man with you. The others will love to hear his fairy tales, just before they rip him apart."

To the stricken, fallen man, she knelt down and grabbed him by the throat. *"I am nobody's servant!"*

His eyes bulged, and he choked on her grip. "Pray for me, little man," snarled the vampire. *"Pray for me!"*

Juliana gathered the food and gave a look of disgust to the two men, whom she recognised now to having frequented the church, which, though in the village, was on the opposite side of the now damaged road.

For just a fleeting moment, Juliana wondered how they had made it into the village. As she walked away from them, she thought *and they think I am in league with the Devil.*

***

As she arrived back at the Inn, the blood which had been dripping from the sign, had thoroughly dried out. Perhaps it was more accurate to say that the blood had seeped into the wood, and would now remain part of the sign's artwork forever.

The pub itself was not open, for it was just past 9:30 in the morning. Still, a commotion could be heard from inside, and Juliana's pace quickened as she neared the establishment.

She hurried through the narrow hallways and crevices of the old building. As she reached what was known to her and her mother, *the mausoleum*, Mariana appeared.

"I'm glad you're here, my girl. Your newest acquisition is being....difficult."

"Acquisition?"

"Well, what would you like to call her?"

"Practise?"

"Really, Juliana, if she was merely practise, she'd be dead already. She is making the most terrible noise. She is unable to push the coffin lid up, and I am certainly not assisting her. This is your mess. Sort it out at once."

"Have you forgotten your part in this, Mother? The girl has nowhere to go. You killed her husband."

"For that, you are most welcome, Juliana."

Juliana observed her mother. She had heard about that a head vampire, once killed, had no further hold over anyone who had been made a vampire. She didn't really believe it, but just the possibility made her think that Mariana was right to stay within the confines of the Inn.

On the many occasions Juliana would go into the town, the day would pass by without incident. But the murmurs were getting louder, complaints were becoming more vocal. The locals, the ones who had so far escaped Juliana's bite, knew that she was responsible for many of the deaths and disappearances of loved ones.

"I have had a few difficulties of my own," replied Juliana. "The locals are getting more restless. More difficult. I may end up killing them all. That's if they don't kill us."

"Is there something you are not telling me, Juliana?"

Mariana would need to be more specific, but it was likely that her own fears matched those of her daughter. Killing an outsider, and making another of them, as one of the undead did present a set of problems Juliana felt ill equipped to deal with.

If the locals whispers turned into real threats; the kind they would carry out, then Juliana, her mother and the newest addition to their group would be in mortal danger. Their immortal status only remained if they avoided the stake. Fire in itself could not hurt them, but if the people decided to burn The Raven down, they would have no shelter. Their place of rest would be at the biggest risk.

The priest from beyond the broken road, was almost certain to be the one causing the biggest trouble. He often commented on Juliana's porcelain-like complexion, that such a thing was far from normal, and how he observed her tiny mouth remained small, even when she spoke.

As if she was hiding something.

Not for long, thought Juliana. *If I kill this priest, they'll probably send another one. Priests are like the plague of locusts mentioned in the Bible. That much, I can agree with.*

She tried to brush the evil thoughts from her mind. She did not care if they got her, but Juliana could not abide anything happening to her mother.

"No," lied Juliana. "Everything is just fine, Mother. I will see to the girl. I'm sorry she has troubled you."

"No trouble," replied her mother. "But if there ever is a repeat, just kill them clean, as I do."

Juliana could not let that go. "Clean? You were the raven when you gored the man's heart out, Mother!"

"Oh Juliana. Forget *clean* then. Just kill them. In any case, you need to find me some more to feed on. I feel a little weak these days. No teenagers, babies or rodents. Strong men. Virile men. Bring them here."

"Of course, Mother."

"Maybe you can open the road again."

"I will."

I just have that priest to deal with, thought Juliana.

To her knowledge, her mother had never killed a man of the cloth. That particular priest had been the head of that church for some twenty years now, and he retained a healthy congregation. His most popular sermons involved the castigating of the Devil's worshippers.

"For He is amongst you. Amongst *us*. Lucifer. Beelzebub. Samael. *Satan*. He is amongst us, my brothers and sisters. Know this; his power gets more and more stronger, each and every day. We must pray to the Lord, first for forgiveness, second for hope, thirdly for the strength to defeat this evil!"

After the mass, the priest would sometimes be asked just *how the evil could be defeated.*

He would offer a cryptic, yet rather standard answer. One that was straight out of the text books.

"Just pray to the Lord, child. Pray to the Lord."

After confession one day, a man took the priest aside. "Father, you say to pray to the Lord, but my wife died last year, despite my many prayers and those of the congregation. You say pray for work, but I have not had a proper job in years. You say to be thankful to the Lord for our health and wealth, but mine is failing me every single day. As for money, I have none."

"You will be needing to return to the confessional, my son." The priest had a wry smile on his face, but this did not betray what he said, as he meant every word.

"Father, you don't understand. You see only what goes on within the confines of these church walls. The landscape of this place is changing. *People* are changing. That Juliana....there are more like her kind, every day. Oh they hide it well, but I know a vampire when I see one."

Yes, the man knew a vampire when he saw one. One night, his wife had left the family home after an argument with him, and went straight to the Inn of the Blood and the Raven. A few heavy drinks later, she was in the arms of the vampire Juliana, who at first seduced her, before bleeding her to the point of death.

She asked her, as she always did, if they wanted to die, or become as she was.

The pretty woman refused to become like Juliana. For her own part, she returned the woman to her home, not to get well, but to die. Any doctors who visited could do nothing for the girl. Prayers could not be heard, as the priest found himself unable to enter the household.

"I will pray for your wife, but not here," said the priest. "I am not welcome here, and the Devil…I can feel his presence."

"What will you pray for?" asked the man. "You've seen her – seen the state she is in. I go to church every Sunday of my life, and this is my reward?"

"I will pray for her soul, and yours," he replied. In his own mind, he could only do one thing, and pray for a quick death for the woman.

This actual event came to pass. Mariana, frustrated with her daughter's feelings about the *humans,* and increasingly frustrated with her entrapment at The Raven, assumed the bird's shape one night, and attempted to enter the woman's bedroom, and give her a final, absolute death.

The priest had left an array of crucifixes with the husband, but in his disagreement with the priest, he removed them from the bedroom.

"Damn things don't work anyway. Pray for a job, I cannot get one. Pray for my wife to get better, she gets worse. What is the point?"

The raven, which had circled many a night outside the woman's bedroom, seized the opportunity, crashing through the window and violently gored the woman's body. The man came rushing into the room, to be confronted by the horror of his wife being torn apart by the beast, as it fed on her flesh.

This was no ordinary bird; it seemed to grow in size as it gorged on her blood.

Finally it turned to the man and swatted him with its wing, knocking him out cold. The beast thought for a moment to feed on him, but he looked weak and haggard from his life. He could not have been more than twenty-six years old, but looked some thirty years older.

As least his wife had tasted *young*.

"My son," said the priest sternly. "The Lord has given you this day. Use it well."

The man nodded and shook the priest's hand, but left without saying anything further. A plan was being thought through, even as he left the churchyard.

"It's time that candle flame became a raging, unstoppable fire."

***

"Lady G? Lady G? Are you not comfortable? It's our best coffin, far more grand in style and comfort that my mother and I use. Whatever is the problem?"

A muffled, yet reasonably clear sound emanated from underneath the casket's heavy lid.

"I cannot get out, damn you!"

Juliana jumped on top of the casket and tapped it with her hands.

"No, you just haven't tried. You're still trying to open it like a human. You are no longer a human. You have thrown off the shackles and inadequacies of that life. I had to learn this way too; the hard way. No-one ever showed me how to open my coffin."

Inside the coffin, the woman knew that things were different. So much time must have passed since she last heard from Juliana. The other vampire, the girl's mother, she assumed, took no notice of her shouting and banging. It was clear that Juliana had returned to deal with her; or had been sent to deal with her.

"Let me out."

"If you are going to behave, then I will. First things first. You have to accept what you are. Otherwise, I cannot help you. Agreed?"

"It would seem so," came the muffled reply.

Juliana jumped down and flipped the lid open with ease.

"You're a vampire now, which means that the old ways are dead to you. You were trying too hard, just like a human. We are so much more than that."

The woman, called Lady G by Juliana because of the letter that hung as a pendant from her neck, sprang up from the coffin.

"So I am learning and seeing. I just thought to rise up, so I did."

"You can do much more than that," said Juliana excitedly. "Tell me, what is it you want right now?"

"I want to kill someone."

"Well, that's a very good start."

"So take me to them," said the newly-made vampire. "Last night, there were scores of them in the pub."

"Not those," said Juliana. "You cannot kill them."

"I don't understand."

"This will be your first evening at The Raven as one of us. You will see things differently, I promise you. Just be patient."

The new vampire sighed. "I still want to kill someone. How about the priest?"

"Not him," ordered Juliana. "I have thought such things myself. It is too obvious to go after him. Besides, even if you were to get him out of that cursed building, he wears one of those infernal crosses around his neck."

"What is the worst that could happen to us, if we were to attack him whilst he is dressed so? It is but a little trinket. I had one myself. When I became like you, I began to see them for what they really are. Trinkets of deceit, making me believe in a false God."

"I agree with you," said Juliana, "but this is neither the time nor the place. Besides, I must have an audience with *Father WhatsHisName*, sooner rather than later. I have different plans for you."

"So long as it involves me feeding on someone. I feel so weak in body, yet so strong in spirit and desire. I want to kill. Now!"

"Okay, okay," said Juliana with more than a hint of exasperation in her voice. "I will send you to a place that satisfies your bloodlust."

With a wave of her hand, the newly made vampire disappeared from view.

Just before the Inn of The Blood and the Raven was set ablaze.

Daughters of the Devil

"Come out and burn, you daughters of the Devil!" shouted the man whose wife had been killed by the Dreymuirs.

"Or stay *inside* and burn!" laughed another man.

Juliana looked around as the flames climbed up the walls of the old public house all too quickly. Both she and her mother would have to leave.

Juliana remained a touch too human for her mother's liking, though the senior vampire would admit to being sentimental about Marcus and Rocco, who they hoped to see again at some point. Her brothers had been sent out to *spread the word, and the way.*

When she had last seen them, she was unsure. She longed to see them again, especially Rocco, who she felt close to, even though he seemed closer to his brother.

There was no time to gather the portraits of her siblings.

"Mother! We have to go!"

But Mariana was reluctant to go.

"If we leave here, they will kill us. If we burn here, we throw off this form, and simply choose another. Isn't that what Marcus and Rocco have done? Isn't that the option you gave that young woman?"

"Yes," said Juliana, "and you know why. They must continue, even if something happens to us."

"You forget your place, my girl. I have been around longer than Time itself. The only reason God created the Heavens and Earth in seven days is because *I* taught him to understand the concept of time. So you see, nothing mere men can do, with their hands or weapons, can scare me."

"Mother, I am scared they would get to me."

"They won't, my child. As you sent that young girl away, I must send you on your way."

"The priest. He is to pay for this. He is the cause of all this."

"You must away to the castle at once, Juliana."

"No! We were hunted out of there before. I can't leave you here at their kind of mercy, Mother. At least send out those who frequent The Raven to save you."

The group that the woman and her husband had been amongst that night may have been human at one time, but now they were vampires. They sniggered at everything the humans had said, because they had been in their position too at one time.

Somehow, there was always something wrong with the set-up in the surroundings of The Blood and the Raven.
A fallen log. An animal laying on the road, sometimes a deer, often a cow and even an elk. All dead. All a ruse to stop newcomers to the town from ever leaving.

The pub had been burned to the ground more times than Mariana could remember, but Juliana never could. Her mother marvelled at her daughter's child-like remembrance of things. Her brothers called it selective memory. Juliana had all to often remind them that they too chose to forget their part in the most awful of deeds.

She had hoped to escape the killings for a while, but make-up would only get her so far. She retained the pallor of the undead. Only under the kind of lighting that the pub offered could she manage a normal looking appearance.

If she ever went out in the day, her death-white complexion scared the younger children, and even though she wore the most magnificent of dresses, which were designed to take the eyes of onlookers away from her face, it was a subterfuge that could not last.

She was eighteen years old in this phase of her existence. She thought she had seen it all from her mother, who had taken the guise of a human female in this phase, but also that of a raven, as if being a female vampire was not terrifying enough.

That was not all. Her mother had been a beast, almost too terrible to describe. She had been mist, a vapour, a fog, and each time she smothered the life out of anyone caught in its vicinity. She had even been a man, often a lord, knight, or nobleman with some such title. Men had much power back in those days, and they used that power to control other men, and seduce women into their trust. Once Mariana tired of them, whatever guise she was in, they died.

People tended to avoid the town now, so Juliana and her mother had to make it difficult for newcomers to leave, once they had entered the place. Of course, The Blood and the Raven was the only pub in town. Juliana had burned down all others within a twenty-mile radius of the place.

Now, the old pub found itself on fire.

"Not for the first time, certainly not for the last," said Mariana as she morphed into bat form and flew clear of the blaze.

One of the men hurled a hand-sized rock into the air, but it missed the bat by some distance, with a devilish laugh coming from the creature.

The vampire bat beat its wings furiously, and rose clear of the burning public house. Those who frequented the pub, and had never left since being *made* by Juliana and her mother; chose this moment to exit the burning lounge, and fed on the men, women and children outside. There were just too many of them, and whilst some of the vampires were beaten back, it delayed only the inevitable.

One by one, the people fell.

On this side of the broken road, the human population of the town was now zero. As things stood, it was completely populated by vampires.

***

Unless she had made a miscalculation, one person local to the town was still alive, and very much human.

Juliana knew where that person was too, and made her way directly to the church.

"Come out, dear Father! I come to confess my sins! I hope your God has given you at least ten lifetimes, for I have much to confess!"

The priest stayed hidden, but Juliana knew one thing about these humans.

"You forget I used to be like you, Father. Come out of there, so I can make you like *me*."

Candle Flickers

"**S**o ends the tale of The Blood and the Raven," said Seth, who sat shivering in the cold.

The candle wax oozed onto Daisy's hand, but she was glad of the heat. "So she kills the priest as well? Except for vampires, there's no-one left in the town? Well, I'll admit you had me going there a few times Seth; and it was more gory than I'd have liked. But I enjoyed it. What about you, Anna? Joel?"

Seth did not acknowledge whether Daisy's assertion was correct. Instead, he stared as Anna sat, her legs crossed, with a stony expression on her face. Joel, bored of all the non-scary stories, lay on his back, his knees bent, his face barely catching the moonlight.

"Anna? What's wrong with you?"

When Anna did not reply, nor made any movement, Daisy marched over and shook Anna by her shoulders, only for a strange scent, one of death to fill the air.

Anna grabbed Daisy by her wrists, but this was to be her last action, as the girl's head loosened, falling backwards, but remained attached at the neck. Daisy screamed silently at first, only for a huge scream to escape from her once she realised her candle flame had flickered out.

Gretchen looked across at Seth, who wore a similar expression to Anna, only he was very much alive.

Seth was still holding his candle, and it illuminated something around her neck. A thin, gold necklace, with a pendant hanging from it in the shape of the letter G.

Daisy screamed again, only to fall over the bent knees of Joel, whose face was turned away from the group for a reason. His expression was of someone who had been in sheer terror in the moments before his life ended.

His eyes had been pulled from their sockets, his teeth smashed, some of them protruding through the skin where his cheekbones were. Two savage bite marks on his neck looked to have been made by some kind of animal. In addition to all this, Joel had been disemboweled, remaining conscious and alive whilst all this had been happening to him.

He would have been fully aware, even though his murder would have taken a matter of seconds, he would have felt every cut, tear, and slash of the beast that killed him. His death was made all the worse because he mocked the entities that filled scary stories.

Now, he would forever be a part of one.

"You tell the story so well, Seth, that Daisy held her gaze on you the whole time. Anna and Joel are like so many, they disbelieve. I hate it when they do that. Just wait a second whilst I get Daisy."

Seth said nothing to Gretchen, but tried hard to remember when he had first come into contact with her. She had said she had been around for two hundred years, but that was impossible, as she looked no older than fifteen years old.

Of course, Gretchen had learned to play her part well. She too was practised in taking many forms, and in this existence, took the part of a teenager in their last year at school.

Whilst he was thinking about this, he was showered with a sticky liquid, too thick to be merely the damp rain in the priory, which had started to seep from the clouds above.

"Sorry about that," said Gretchen, who had returned with Daisy, half her insides hanging outside of her body. "She's a strong one, I'll say that for her."

Gretchen ripped Daisy's arm out of her shoulder and tossed it towards Seth, the dismembered limb landing just in front of his crossed legs.

"I don't want it, but maybe you do," said Gretchen. "All that story telling must have made you hungry. Her arms are too skinny for me. Good job she has – *had*, a big chest."

Seth remained silent, disgusted with himself for being part of these seditious acts.

"You're not hungry? Or are you sulking, Seth?"

He spoke, but only after he had spoken the question in his head over and over again.

"How many more times do we have to do this?"
"What do you mean?" asked Gretchen, between mouthfuls of Daisy.

"When will this end?"

Gretchen paused her consumption of Daisy.

"It never ends. *Never*. Since I was made like this, I have always been hungry. Know that it will never end Seth. Your reward for bringing them to me is a good night's rest."

Seth stood up, and followed Gretchen out of the priory. The lifting of the curse would simply have to wait for another day.

Gretchen spoke to him just one more time, but it was a line he was familiar with.

"Tomorrow, we'll find a new group of people to tell your story to."

Author Reflections

The Blood and the Raven is rather like a 'story within a story'. You have the legend of the story itself, and Seth is the eyes and mouthpiece of the tale.

His is a tragic story. He is forced by the vampire, ultimately revealed as Gretchen – *the woman* in the story, and *Lady G* as she is later referred – to find a succession of people to find, so that she can feed on them.

She won't kill him – not while he is useful anyway. But can he kill her? What would happen if he does? Will Gretchen, and *Juliana* – our anti-heroine in Murderous Little Darlings - meet again?

With vampire lore, there is much scope for the author. This is the second of seven short novellas, that will tie up together at the close of book seven.

I rather doubt that will end my association with vampires. I enjoy these characters. Whilst I am sorry for Daisy's demise in this story, Gretchen's ruthless manner of killing, in a way, has to be admired.

Why can't Gretchen go on her own, and kill without Seth's help? Well, it would draw too much attention to her, and she is able to cover her tracks – something that is alluded to in the first Tale of Vampires.

Does the priest survive an encounter with Juliana? You'll find out soon enough.

Innocent While She Sleeps

Inspiration for
Innocent While She Sleeps

Does a vampire truly sleep, when at rest in their coffin? In this story, without seeking to humanise the vampires involved, I wanted to explore the *psyche* of the vampire, should the creature actually have one.

It seems reasonable to me that a creature that was human at one time, would retain a small shred of its humanity. After all, they would take a human guise in order to fit in around others.

Around those they wished to kill.

When I watched vampire movies as a child, especially the Hammer Horror films, vampires could be found in their coffins, almost serene in their appearance.

Of course, this was usually a prelude to one of the film's protagonists attacking the vampire while they lay in their coffins. In this story, I wanted to explore what a vampire might be thinking as they rested.

A vampire's day often consisted of several kills, and even though they would sometimes sit down to a meal, and eat as humans would, it was more a case of going through the motions than anything else.

Perhaps they liked these daily human rituals more then they would care to admit.

That is where the similarity ends, for end it must. A vampire is a *significantly* different creature to a mere human.

Unless they are killed, they remain immortal. They drain the blood, and often, the life, from those unfortunate enough to cross their path.

The vampires in my stories will not romance another person. They will not enter into idle chatter, and even though they kill, they cannot be dismissed as being one-dimensional entities.

They are to be feared, and at the same time, respected.

We should be thankful they remain fictional.

No Rest for the Wicked

H er footsteps made no sound on the ground as she walked.

The cobble-stoned footpath, which widened out towards a humpback bridge, led to the only building left standing on that side of town. The ash and dust had settled on the Inn of the Blood and the Raven.

Only the church remained.

The vampire's threats had turned out to be just that. *Threats*. The priest remained safe within the church of St Peter and St Paul. He would not hear her approach, not this time, nor at any time before. Inside the church, he had readied many barriers, though he knew full well that they were only the kind of barriers that kept humans from entering.

What the priest was dealing with, was anything but human.

When she walked, it was not always when the night was at its blackest. It was a kind of half-night, with the sky not betraying whether it was dusk or dawn. Still, in these small hours, she would appear to be wandering aimlessly, yet in truth, there were only two places she could go. Ahead, to the church, or even further ahead, to the Castle Dreymuir, which housed the soil that nourished her while she would sleep.

Knowing only one reason to exist – to feed on human blood; the vampire was troubled as she lay in rest. Images of those she had killed, so many of them, *so many*, began to haunt her. Then, as the time came for her to rise from her slumber, she would forget all the evil deeds she had committed.

There was one other entity who had, unknown to the vampire, been observing her behaviour. This was not a vampire at rest, for Juliana would rise, sometimes at 2am, or 3am, sometimes when the clock struck four, or perhaps five. But resting for hours at a time was no longer something she was able to do.

The one who rested with her in the mausoleum had been just eight years old when she had been made into a vampire. She had been given no choice in the matter. Juliana's brothers had been there when it happened.

They had called her 'a gift'. At the time, she had not known what they had meant by that. Their description of her as a gift was sickening to her now. But on that day, her existence as she knew it had died.

Over the time that had passed, she had observed that Juliana took little pleasure in finding a victim. She preferred her victims to be placed right in front of her. Then, she would move in, quick-as-thought, before draining almost every last drop of blood from their body.

If she took a liking to them, she would offer them death, or a chance at a new way of living.

But the little girl had not been given any choice. Juliana took her blood, leaving just enough to become one of them. The newly made vampire learned quickly, and within moments of her new existence, she followed Juliana into the sky, joining her mother in the form of vampire bats.

They hadn't meant to catch Juliana's brothers, Marcus and Rocco. That could wait for another day.

All the same, the little vampire, *Nina*, was now stuck in a small girl's body, whilst Juliana and her mother could execute different forms without restrain.

This was the fifth night in a row that Nina had heard Juliana rise up from her coffin. It was not the kind of sound that a human could hear. You would have to be a vampire to know, and those that knew how to do such things, would not tell others how to do them.

Nina could tell Juliana had returned. On this occasion, she was brave enough to rise from her own coffin, only to see Juliana completely ignore her, and return to her slumber.

Even then, that was not the end of it. Nina could hear Juliana mumbling in her sleep, with various names being mentioned. Some of them, she knew, of course, because on occasion, Juliana would take Nina with her into the town.

It was under the pretence of shopping, but many of the locals knew different. Juliana knew what they were thinking too; so she would look for someone who was maybe from London, or further North.

"Just wait here, Nina," Juliana would say. Then, she would chat, *oh so briefly*, to the one who took her fancy. On that morning, it was a young boy, of maybe no more than fifteen years of age.

"I couldn't possibly come along with you, my lady," said the boy politely. "You are older than me, and well, I don't know about such things."

"So I'll *teach* you about such things," smiled Juliana.

That - was pretty much *that*. The boy, or whoever it happened to be, would follow Juliana wherever she happened to go. Sometimes, if it was early in the day, it was back to the castle. Other times, it was at bars and restaurants like these.

Juliana ushered the boy into the ladies restrooms. He looked as if he wanted to protest, but there were none alive to say they had protested against Juliana with a modicum of success. Then she would fix her gaze on him, capturing him under her wicked spell, before sinking her teeth into his flesh. He would cry out, but no-one could hear him. There was far too much hustle and bustle in the town for anyone to hear him.

When she had finished, she took a napkin from his coat pocket, and dabbed her mouth and lips until they were dry. Then she was ready to go. She would collect Nina, and if she had fed enough for one day, they would return to the castle. Juliana laughed as she could hear the screams in the distance.

"I suppose he's been found. Oh well, gives them a story to tell their friends, doesn't it? I'd show you how I do it, so you could learn. But you don't want to learn, do you Nina?"

Nina shook her head.

"Say it, Nina. Come on! Say it! Say you don't want to be like your evil Juliana."

"That's right. I don't want to be like you."

"*We are what we are, and we do what we do*," said Juliana. "You may not believe that right now, but one day, I promise that you will. Oh look, Nina! Look!"

An uncharacteristic grunting sound escaped from Nina, before she added with exasperation; "What is it now? I just want to go back to the castle."

"It's more practise," smiled Juliana, who started to skip ahead of Nina.

Nina observed a woman, who was provocatively dressed, disappear down the corner of a street to her left. The lighting was poor, but the woman paused under the only street lamp that was lit on the entire road.

A man who had seen far too many summers approached the woman, and asked her *how much*.

Before the woman had the opportunity to give an answer, Juliana appeared in front of the man, and knocked him to the ground. "If I ever see you around here again, I'll kill you if it's the last thing I do."

The man gathered himself to his feet, cursed at Juliana, and ran away as fast as his legs would carry him.

"Lady, what are you doing?" asked the woman, whose chest was almost escaping from her dress. "That was my week's money tonight. You're not the police, are you?"

"No," said Juliana, slowly turning to face the woman, who at twenty-five was older than Juliana appeared to be. "I don't follow the laws that mere men set. Let me make it up to you. I'm rich, you know. I was only going to ask you the same question he did."

"No," said the woman, who could barely disguise the discomfort in her voice. "No girls. I don't suffer women. I have a rule about that."

"You will suffer me," said Juliana. "I do not follow the rules that women set either."

"What do you want, then?" The woman's composure was all but gone.

"Your blood."

Juliana pushed the woman against the wall, before consuming her blood, gorging on her to the point that she could take no more. The dark red fluid splattered onto the cobbled street.

She placed her two little fingers in her mouth, and whistled. Nina was scared as two black hounds bounded towards Juliana, who patted both dogs on the heads, then pointed to the body of the stricken girl.

"Feeding time, boys. Aren't I good to you?"

She left them to tear the girl's body apart. Her mother, the vampire Mariana, would be pleased that Juliana had at long last learned to *clean up her mess.*

"Come on Nina, we'll go back to the castle now. I'd have offered you the girl, but like you said, you're not interested. Oh, the things you miss out on!"

Nina fought the temptation to comment. Juliana would simply dismiss anything she said anyway, so she said nothing. But things were going to change, they could not stay the same forever.

Mariana may have managed to elude decapitation for centuries, but Nina did not believe that good fortune would extend to Juliana. She was making too many errors, for all blood spilt left a trail. Juliana's arrogance would trip her up one day. Nina did not merely wish for that day to come, she wanted to do all she could to make it happen.

Another night in the castle, and Juliana continued to be restless. Nina decided that before the morning sun broke, she would have to act.

Child of Satan

The priest looked up at one of the *Via Crucis*, the Stations of the Cross, and blessed himself not once, but three times. He was observing the 5th Station, where Simon of Cyrene assisted Jesus with the carrying of the cross.

As he was unable to leave the church for fear of his own safety, he cursed himself for his cowardice. Even if it was not observed by others, it was still cowardice.

The three-hundred and fifty-year-old church was a haven of peace. It had a strong congregation of three hundred people. *Had.*

Just a few months earlier, *the faithful* had all been killed, or turned into vampires. The priest shook his head, and looked to the floor ahead of him.

"Truly, these are Godless times," he said, sadness weighing down his every word.

He blessed himself again. He found fear threatening to overwhelm him. If she came for him, there was little he could do to stop her. Her kind were not supposed to be able to breach a House of God. They would have to be welcomed over the threshold, so went the convention.

For this creature, there would be no welcome. But she was unlikely to be bound by convention.

"They are what they are, and they will do what they will do," said the priest out loud.

He gripped the cross in front of his chest and felt confidence renew within him.

"So I must do, what I must do."

Darkness fell through the stainless glass windows, and even though the church was never the warmest of places, the temperature was dropping rapidly. The priest's belief was being tested. He felt his heart rate quicken; pea-sized beads of sweat appeared upon his brow. His arms tensed up, whilst his hands shook uncontrollably. With clammy fingers he grasped at the cross on his chest, only for it to slip from his hand, clattering to the floor. He quickly retrieved it, for he knew he was not alone.

The vampire was with him.

She had averted her eyes from the many crosses that surrounded her. She was in extreme discomfort, being in this place. But it was a case of one-on-one, because, for her, God did not exist. At least, not in a manner that could harm her.

The priest's footsteps, however, could be heard. As he made his way towards her, his legs felt like chocolate melting in the sun. He wondered if this was how Jesus felt when approaching Golgoltha.

Serenely, she sat in one of the pews, waiting for him to approach her. She was not frightened of him; for he represented no threat to her.

He regarded her. Dark, shoulder length hair, hidden under a pastel blue woolen hat. She wore a coat of the same colour. Her short legs dangled over the bench, and she playfully kicked at the pew in front of her.

"Little girl, in the name of God, tell me, why are you here?"

Nina turned her head to face him. She smiled, her death-white pallor unable to betray that her youth, her life, had been taken from her.

"I'm here to *help* you, Father." The little vampire seemed most sincere with her words.

She stood up from the pew, and yet, kept her distance from the priest. "Though we cannot talk whilst you hold *that* in front of me. Put it away, Father. Please."

The priest was reluctant to follow her instruction. There was an uneasy stand off.

"I did say *please*."

The priest sighed heavily, and placed the cross under his vestments.

"May God protect me, and may God have mercy on your soul."

"Regarding your first point, it's a bit late for that," said Nina. "I'm not so concerned about the second part either."

"*Child of Satan*! Why are you here?"

Showing no sign of being upset by the priest's curt words, Nina spoke gently. "Oh, come on now, Father. There's no need to be rude. I told you why I am here. I'm here to help you."

The priest placed his hand over his chest and felt the outline of the cross underneath his clothes.

"You can leave this place and never return!"

"So much for the God who loves unconditionally," Nina tut-tutted.

"I can leave, yes. But you cannot, can you Father? Because you are alone. Go outside, and Juliana will kill you. She told you so herself, didn't she?"

"She could be saved, as you could be, child."

"Then we are not so different in our thinking, are we Father? Do you know that I have not killed?"

"It does not matter. Whilst you side with the Father of Lies, it does not matter. You and the creatures that reside in that castle are damned."

"Will you not help me, Father? Will you not pray for me? I am no more than I appear to be. A simple little girl."

"Enough of these games! In the name of the Fath-"

Before he could complete his holy instruction, Nina hissed at the priest, and the cross underneath his clothes became engulfed in flames. He cried out in pain, and the cross fell from him, charred and bent by the heat of the fire.

"A simple little girl with some extraordinary powers," continued Nina. "We can help each other, Father. *We can help each other.*" Nina extended a small hand to the priest. He grabbed it, and shuddered.

"Cold, aren't I?" laughed Nina. "Yeah, it does that. Never mind. Anyway, I've been at Castle Dreymuir a while now. How long, I cannot remember. It's possible my real mother is dead. I do not have the bloodlust; not in the same way that the ones you know as Mariana and Juliana possess."

She paused, expecting the priest to say something in reply, or offer a retort, but nothing was forthcoming, so she continued.

"I would like to return to things as they once were, but maybe I cannot do that," said Nina, almost sounding sad as she spoke.

"I expect too, that you would like to be able to leave this place, be free to come and go as you please. Maybe even build a new congregation, right Father?"

"Yes," he nodded. "I would like to leave. But you and I both know that she will attack me. It would seem that even here, God has forsaken me. Indeed, the Devil's power is great."

"Now you're speaking my language," smiled Nina. "At least you and I are on the same page."

"And what are the words written on this page?"

"Little Nina was avenged, as the ones who made her a vampire lay with a stake in their chests, fleas and maggots feasting on their rotting corpses. Their heads lay separated from their bodies, and those hateful creatures had their eyes ripped out by the ravens who once feared them."

"What is this? You want the Dreymuir women killed?"

"Not women, Father. They're not even human. *They are already dead.* The question is, are you prepared to do what is necessary?"

"Why would you want them to die?"

Nina's eyes darkened. "Do I look *well* to you, Father? The scent of your blood hangs heavy in the air. It *calls* to me. I am a vampire, Father, but I did not have a choice in the matter. I have wanted vengeance ever since. Now, I see an opportunity, and I will not let it fall from my grasp, as easily as the cross that fell from your hand. But if you don't help me, I fear I will become a greater monster than those that have made me."

"Child, what are you saying? You do not want to kill?"

"Oh, no, Father. I do. I do have the bloodlust, and it is more powerful than anything you have in this place. I could snap your neck and back like you are nothing; and you know it too. I will kill - today, tomorrow, someday. Unless you help me."

"I cannot help you! I cannot leave here. I am alone!"

"You are not alone, Father, not completely. What about the convent three miles north?"

With all the other worries on his mind, the priest had forgotten about that. But even so, what could nuns do against vampires? He sensed the girl was deceiving him, yet her words troubled him. Yet she seemed sincere in her wanting to leave the life of the vampire behind.

"What about it?"

"Do we have an agreement, or not, Father? You will help me, and I will help you. Agreed?"

The priest felt he really was making a deal with the Devil. But to be rid of the Dreymuirs, that would be an opportunity too big to pass on.

"You need one of the nuns to visit the Castle," said Nina. "Do not have them arrive in the traditional garb of the heathen God."

"You would use those women as bait! I will not send them to their death. You are tricking me, daughter of Satan, and *you are not welcome here*."

With that last sentence, Nina could no longer maintain her presence in the church. She disappeared from view. The priest found he had the shakes once again; but he retained the presence of mind to stumble into the vestry, constantly blessing himself and praising God for surviving an encounter with a vampire.

In a small cabinet lay an array of bottles. The priest took one out, along with a glass, then decided to not use the glass at all. He placed one hand on top of the cabinet to steady himself, then gulped the glass of potcheen down in one go.

He knew the vampire was right. There would be no leaving the church, as Juliana had already threatened to kill him, and there was no doubt she would succeed.

Unless he did something that went against everything that he stood for and believed in.

Unless he chose to *trust* the vampire.

The Blood is the Life

"How is she?" asked Mariana.

"Hmm?" Juliana barely looked up from her food. "Who?"

"Oh, dear girl, you know who. *Nina*."

"*How is she*? How would I know? I care not."

"You need to care. If you don't manage this now, we could have a lot of problems later. I am not ready to return to the *new* Inn. Things need to calm down a little, and time helps people forget. The town will soon be populated once again. In the meantime, take her under your wing."

"If you say so, Mother."

"*I do say*. As for the girl, she looks rather gaunt. Have you not found her anyone yet? You spend hours out with her, and while you look fine, she looks like Death itself. I'm also not lost on how ironic that is."

Juliana shoved her plate away.

"She will not feed. She will not kill. What would you have me do with her?"

Mariana placed her fork down beside her plate, before jamming her knife into the meat on the table. She knew Juliana had resisted *the life* as well. Perhaps this had been passed to Nina when Juliana made her a vampire.

"She is impossible!"

"No, my dear daughter. *You* were impossible. She is being merely difficult. Perhaps you need to treat her more like one of the family."

"I cannot – I *will not* think of her as my sister! This is all Marcus and Rocco's fault! When are you going to deal with them?"

"All in good time," replied Mariana. "Do not change the subject, Juliana. Just make the girl like your little sister."

"No!"

"It was not a request. Besides, you are looking plump, Juliana. Get her to feed on you a little. The blood is the life, remember that."

"Why are you so keen to get her up to speed, Mother? What are you up to?"

Mariana hoped Juliana would do well in her stead. In the last few days when she left the castle, Mariana observed that the priest had been teasing her; shamelessly walking about the church graveyard. He almost looked to be inviting her to attack. He was getting his courage from somewhere. Mariana believed he was getting reinforcements. She would have to do the same, but that meant leaving Juliana for a while, and she did not know when she would return.

She dabbed her lips with a napkin and stood up from her chair.

"I am *up* to protecting you, child. That's all I exist for."

She wrapped a headscarf around her, and cupped Juliana's chin with her hand.

"Get her to feed."

"When will you return?"

"When I *return*, Juliana. Hold the fort until then."

With that, Mariana left the castle silently and effortlessly.

Juliana pushed her chair back, and decided to carry out her mother's orders.

"Nina. Nina! Where are you?"

Juliana walked through a number of doors and corridors, calling out to the little girl. The castle echoed Juliana's voice, but apart from that, there was total silence.

"Nina, show yourself. Now."

Juliana stopped walking and turned around, only for the little girl to appear in front of her.

"Pretty good at this, aren't I?"

"Not nearly good enough," said Juliana, feeling outsmarted but not outdone. She grabbed her hand.

"Come with me Nina. This will be fun."

Juliana ushered Nina into her bedroom. It was a huge room, with a four poster bed that was rarely, if ever used. Sometimes, when her rest was troubled, she would go to this room, lay on the bed for a while, and feel the soft furnishings on the bed warm her cold skin. Knowing it was all a façade, she would wander again, until it was time to return to her coffin.

Nina knew it too, but did not want to alert Juliana to the fact. She had to play along if things were going to turn out the way she wanted them to.

"It's a lovely room, Juliana. A pity we cannot draw the curtains back."

Juliana surprised Nina by what she did next. She pushed the drapes back, just enough to let light through. It illuminated the far side of the room, to where a huge wardrobe stood.

Juliana rushed over to it and pulled the doors open.

"Here you are Nina, look at these."

Nina peered inside, and could see an array of dresses of all colours, styles and designs. Her own dress was brown, pinafore length, with a lace trim. It looked dowdy in comparison to what she saw.

"You can wear any of these except the purple. That's my colour."

Nina looked at Juliana, who wore a red dress and a black robe.

"My *favourite* colour, Nina. I don't choose to wear it every day."

Juliana pulled out a yellow dress, and held it in front of Nina.

"With your black hair and hazel eyes – well – I can tell they are hazel even if no-one else can – this will really work for you. Come on Nina, put it on."

Nina had to admit she liked the dress. But her feelings of joy, which she should have had, escaped her. She felt disinterested in everything. Only one thing drove her, to see her mother again. Nina estimated that seven years had passed since she had seen her, and if she was to ever see her again, Juliana, her brothers, *and* her mother would have to die.

"Are we like sisters now? This is a gift?"

"Yes. You can think of it like that. It's a gift."

Acting the big sister role was not coming easily to Juliana. She didn't care for Nina, and she resented her mother for leaving her alone with the troublesome little girl.

"It's a little girl's dress," said Nina. "I want to wear the kind of dresses you wear. But thanks to you, I'll never get to do that. I'll never have a body like yours."

Juliana laughed. "Well of course you can. When you have more energy, you can take practically any form you would like. Including mine."

"It won't be the same. I could make my body look like yours, but it won't be mine. It will be a charade. A shell. A *nothing*."

"When we are bats, we don't really know what it is like to be a bat. We just take the form. That's all we're doing, Nina. Don't get so hung up on it."

Nina flung herself onto the bed and began to wail. Juliana hushed her, not liking the sound at all.

"If you want to be treated like a grown-up, you should act like one."

"I don't want to be a grown-up!"

"Then be what you are," said Juliana, fed up with Nina's playacting. "Be a vampire. Hold out for as long as you can. But you can't deny what you are. You are a killer, and you will kill one day. It is just a matter of time."

Nina buried her head into the bedclothes. Juliana grabbed her wrist, only for Nina to choose that moment to turn around, slashing Juliana's wrist with a little knife that came out from nowhere.

Blood splattered onto the yellow dress, droplets of the crimson fluid creating blotches on the wooden floor.

"I'll kill you!" screamed Nina. "I will bloody kill you!"

Juliana clasped a hand over her wrist to stop the bleeding, then took it away once more.

"No. You won't kill me. But you will taste my blood. You haven't fully embraced your vampire side, Nina. It's long overdue."

"Noooo!"

Nina tried to get away, but Juliana was far too strong, and pinned Nina by her wrists to the bed. Her grasp was too much for the weakened vampire, and Nina limply surrendered the knife, stained with Juliana's blood.

Juliana held her wrist over Nina's mouth, but she turned her face away, refusing to let droplets of blood enter her mouth.

"The blood is the life, Nina. Come on, drink up."

"No," she whimpered. "I don't want to become like you."

Juliana refused to be deterred. In the haze, torturous images of those she had killed haunted her once more. Even those she had made a vampire, like Gretchen, taunted her. But they were just fleeting images, and though Nina kicked out wildly, she was no match for Juliana, who pinched the girl's nose with one hand, forcing her mouth open.

One after another, droplets of blood laced the inside of Nina's mouth.

Nina was a vampire, but she had resisted killing all this time. That night, her plan to involve the priest had not been the only thing to die.

Cast No Shadow

The priest hurried from the church, and refused to look behind him, for fear that the vampire was tracking him. It didn't matter which one it was. Mariana, Juliana, or the little girl who had the gall to see him in the church; would all be efficient at killing.

As he walked, he continued to bless himself. One time, he had an audience with the Pope, who told him that 'you cannot die whilst blessing yourself.'

"Maybe not, Your Holiness, but I think your words will be tested this night," he said to himself.

He lamented how the town used to be. Bustling with people, thriving businesses, until the evil came. Now, any person he could meet on his way to the convent could be one of *Them*.

Even the sound of a bird flapping its wings in the air above terrified him. One could not tell on a cloudy day, if it was a bird above, or a vampire bat. His laboured steps quickened apace once more.

Even though the convent was just two miles walk away from the church, as the gradient of the road turned uphill, the priest found his pace slowing once again, and his chest tightened a little. Shadows from the tree branches above loomed large over him, the wind whistled through the leaves with accusations.

Accusations that were almost certainly imagined by the priest, but they felt all too real to him.

The convent was on the highest point of a hill overlooking the cities of Birmingham to the south, and Derby to the north. Even though Castle Dreymuir was five miles away from the grounds of the convent, one of the nuns kept a watchful eye in its direction. Indeed, a one of them would take turns to keep watch on the place, not just at night-time, but also in the day.

The road ahead narrowed, the sky began to fall dark, and rain pelted the priest from above. It was fine rain, the kind that would soak you right through to the bone, even though it appeared to be too fine to do so.

The priest could hear his own footsteps. He could discern other sounds, like the rustling of his overcoat. As the fine rain soaked in, his hat would tilt down towards his eyebrows, forcing him to take an ungloved hand out of his pocket to push the brim upwards again. He had not brought an umbrella, as he wished to see at all times what was in front of him, but also what he had left behind. He had remembered to lock the church and even emptied the tabernacle.

Although he had waited on the nuns to visit him to bring the holy bread and wine, they had not done so this week, and it troubled him greatly. His mind started to race ahead of himself. He wondered if the vampires had breached the walls of the convent, and turned those nuns into vampires, or killed them outright.

He had to go to find out. He had to know for sure. There was *no two roads about it*, as his mother used to say. Staying in the church was no longer an option. They would find a way to get to him. He was finding courage within himself that he did not know existed.

That soon left him as he continued his ascent up the winding and steep hill. There had been much discussion in the old days about whether it actually was a hill or a mountain. Successive tests had revealed it to be two hundred feet short of being a mountain. The priest was thankful for anything that eased the journey to the convent.

Ahead of him, some two hundred yards away, was something that stood between the priest and safe passage to the convent.

It stood motionless, and the priest let out a nervous laugh, called for The Lord a few times, and soon became as still as his quarry.

A goat.

A goat with red eyes, that burned its stare directly at him. The priest half expected the goat to say something. But he knew the creature had links with devil worship. The priest tried in vain not to look scared, and took one pace towards the goat.

For its part, the goat matched the priest's action, then waited for his next move. The priest found himself unable to walk in a straight line, and veered off at an angle. The goat matched him, move-for-move; the red colour in its eyes appeared to deepen in intensity.

"You demon, Mariana Dreymuir! Is it you? Move, you wicked beast!"

The priest tried to sound commanding, but far from backing off, the goat changed tack, and bounded towards the priest. It changed its form into a hound, and leaped at the priest, its jaw wide open, its teeth laid bare.

He knew he could not outrun the beast. The priest crouched down, and waited for the hellhound to consume him. The scent of the beast was overpowering, and he passed out from the smell of burning flesh, which he believed was his own.

"Dear God, please don't forsake me," were the last words uttered from his mouth.

***

"*Definitely* one of the vampires," said the nun watching the proceedings from afar. Using a rudimentary telescope to see the events unfold, it was hard to tell if the beast had made a kill. "It would appear to have gone, Sister," affirmed the young nun. "We should go to him."

"No, I would not do that," replied the other nun, who was more senior to the young girl. "Whatever attacked him could still be out there."

"But if it is the priest-"

"We must leave him there," she interjected. "It is not safe to venture out. Look how quick the dark has fallen. Evil casts no shadow, especially in the dark."

"Sister-" she implored, but found herself being dismissed.

"I believe I have made the position clear. You, I, in fact - *nobody* from here is to go to that man. Priest or not, we must leave him. I am sorry."

The older nun placed a motherly hand on the girl's shoulder, but said no more. The young girl sighed and said a prayer for the man.

She waited one more hour, and decided to leave the convent as quietly as she could. Before anyone could suspect anything, she would return. Knowing she would be in trouble with the Sisters was the least of her concerns.

***

She hurried down the road towards the stricken man. She had the good sense to bring an oil lamp with her that lit the way ahead.

Good. He was still there, and had not moved at all; the imprint of his image through the lens had stayed on her since leaving the convent. The other nuns at the convent would not understand why she had to go to him. But they would when she returned.

Whilst she pondered just how she was going to bring him to the convent, it was her good fortune that a car trundled along towards them in the darkness. The lights from the car illuminated the road.

The driver pulled onto the far side of the road and inquired as to what was the problem. When the young nun told him, he suggested going to a doctor, though admitted finding one so late at night might be a problem.

The nun told him not to worry, that she only wished to return to the convent with the priest so that the sisters could attend to him. The man was more than happy to oblige, and soon enough, the nun was able to call for assistance.

The nun who had replaced her on the night watch hurried down the stairs.

"Annabelle! Do you know how much trouble you will be in when Sister catches up with you?"

"She wouldn't go to him," replied the young nun. "Sarah, please, just help me to help him. You will, won't you?"

Sarah did not wish to encounter the wrath of the Sister either. But as it was the priest of the local church, she agreed that Annabelle was right, and these were a special set of circumstances.

The two young nuns brought the man in, and seeing he was unconscious but breathing, were concerned, but also relieved.

"He's going to be alright," said Sarah happily. "But we won't be, not when Sister catches up with us."

"Oh, you know Sister," smiled Annabelle. "She always loves the priest to visit. She should be thanking us really."

"She won't thank us, Annabelle. I was to keep watch after you, and I was only in the next room when you left – right after Sister gave you a warning."

"I know Sarah, I know. Thanks for looking out for me. I will attend to Father now. Good night."

"Good night Annabelle. Remember what I said, will you? If he wakes up, give him the bread and wine we have prepared, and send him on his way. Sister won't appreciate any shocks or surprises."

Annabelle nodded gratefully and watched Sarah leave the room.

As she removed the dog collar from the priest, and felt around his neck, two bumps, caused by deep bites into his neck, were probed by her fingers.

"I suppose Sister won't like this surprise *either*," she shuddered.

Innocence Lost

I t had been three long days since Nina had tasted Juliana's blood.

Nina had taken to hiding in narrow passageways and corridors in the castle. *Furious* with Juliana, she point-blank refused to talk to her.

Nina, for her part, was shaking violently; crying uncontrollably at times. At all other times, she let Juliana know in no uncertain terms what she thought of her.

"Nina! Come on! Come on out! I'm not angry with you. I just want to help. I didn't know where you were last night. But I wanted to thank you. I slept very well. Just wanted you to know."

Nina refused to come out of hiding, but Juliana knew where she was at all times. After all, she was well practised in this game. Her brothers Marcus and Rocco knew that Juliana was extremely good at hiding herself.

Until she needed to reveal her hiding place, Nina would no doubt stay hidden. Juliana smiled, because she could see through the walls. Nina would learn this skill in time, but Juliana enjoyed having the upper hand for once. Dealing with her mother always meant that she was always second best. When Nina finally came out of hiding, she reminded Juliana of this fact.

"Nina! Do sit down. I always set a place for you at the table. It hasn't been the same without you."

"Don't make fun of me. I'm still very angry with you."

"Nina, that meat is bloody as hell. And it was detached from its owner a good while ago. Eat it. I don't want anything happening to you whilst Mother is away."

"Hmmph!" exclaimed Nina as she sat down. "I expect she'll be as angry at you as I am, for what you did to me."

"What I *did* to you?"

"You trapped me in this body."

Juliana put her fork down and glared at Nina.

"Trapped you? What on earth are you going on about?"

"There's no point telling you. Don't you know, Juliana, that you've got what I would call *selective memory*? It's so easy for you to blank out the awful things you have done, and blame it on a lack of rest. You know full well what you did, what you've done, what you're doing. Just like you knew what you were doing when you poured your own blood into *me*."

Juliana sat back in her chair as if Nina had said the worst thing in the world.

"Well, there's just no pleasing some people. You were ill, Nina. You needed blood. Mother did not want anything to happen to you. So I did, what anyone else would do."

"You didn't have to make me like you, knowing full well I can *never* be like you!"

"I still don't know what you're talking about."

Nina stood up and twirled around in her dress. "You see this? You see it, don't you?"

Juliana observed Nina in the pretty dress, one she had wore herself some ten years before.

"I see it. What's wrong with it? Knowing you, you would find fault with the Moon itself."

"Not the dress. *Me*. Now look at you, you can't fit into this dress, can you?"

"Get to the point, Nina."

"You look eighteen years old, if not older, Juliana. But I will never be eighteen. Not truly. I had a life, I had friends, I had my mother, and you stole that from me. You and your bastard brothers!"

"Nina!" Juliana found herself actually suffering from shock at the girl's harsh words. "Nina, look - you can change your form, you can make your body like mine if you want to. It is a gift we vampires have. You should embrace it."

"I don't *want* to embrace it. Even if I could do that, as you say, it wouldn't be real. It would be a fantasy. The reality is – I will never see my mother again, and I will never grow up to be a young woman. Or an old woman. You stole that from me. Nothing is real if you don't believe in who you are. I look at myself, and I see something else, something which is abhorrent to me. Do you have any idea, any understanding, of what you have done to me?"

"I'm not going to apologise, if that's what you're after," remarked Juliana. "What then? Should I have killed you, when I had the chance?"

"No. But you should have killed *your* mother, and gave us *all* a chance."

Juliana launched herself at Nina, grabbed her throat and pinned her against the wall. Nina made no attempt to fight it, such was the fury in Juliana's eyes. Nina expected it was this kind of expression people saw just before Juliana killed them.

"No wonder you're haunted at night. You look so innocent when you sleep. Like an angel. But you are anything but an angel, Juliana. You may be able to change form. You may be able to traverse time. But you can't outrun your fate."

Juliana's expression softened, and her grip relaxed.

"I don't want to kill you, Nina. Our kind do not harm one another. Sit down, and I will tell you something you didn't know."

Nina did not trust Juliana, but if there was an opportunity to kill her, Juliana had not taken it. She never showed any sign of remorse over her kills.

"I never knew my real mother," said Juliana. "My brothers and I lived together for a while. I do recall sharing time with them here in the castle. But I also remember a time when it was just the three of us, and we would play games with each other, and play tricks on each other. You do know by now that Devil's greatest trick was to convince the world he did not exist? Well, when my brothers and I would play *Vampires*, my trick was to convince them that they didn't exist. Unfortunately, sometimes I could not keep to the plan, and the mask would slip. It was my brothers who would often get me out of trouble, and take the hit for me."

"Why?" scowled Nina. "Because they were scared of you?"

Juliana shook her head. "Because I was their sister. I *am* their sister. I will always be their sister."

"The two boys we were chasing, over the hills of the cemetery?" asked Nina. "Just when I had been bitten by you? Those were your brothers, those are the ones you pretend to love?"

"I didn't say that exactly, did I? I said they would take the hit for me. At least they showed their love. For my part, I showed my merciful side by letting them go. I convinced Mother it was the right thing to do. I wanted to give them the chance that was not afforded to me."

"You keep calling that person your Mother, and yet you say you didn't know your real mother. What happened to your real mother?"

"I was too young to recall all the details of that time. But we learned, my brothers and I, that our *real* mother, the one who had given birth to us, had died whilst giving birth. Giving birth to *me*, in fact. Apparently it all went rather well for Marcus and Rocco. It turned out that *I* was the complication."

"That's putting it mildly," snapped Nina crisply.

"Anyway, we were put in a care home. Social care, if you will. Marcus, ever the trickster, would play *vampire* more often than the other children would like. He'd make it a bit too real, pretending he had slit his throat whilst using tomato juice for blood. He didn't have to do much to convince others that he had fangs. His teeth always looked like that.

He scared the other children so much, that the three of us were kept separate from the other children. Fifteen in all, I think there were. The care workers still had to deal with us though. They had a name for us. It followed us around too. *Murderous Little Darlings*, that's what they used to call us. It was ironic that even up until that point, we hadn't murdered anyone."

"So not ironic then, but prophetic, right?" Nina found herself to be genuinely interested in the story, so kept her questions brief.

"You can infer that if you wish. Anyway, one day, we evaded those carers, who kept a not-so-watchful eye on us, and left the house one night. A game of hide and seek, only two of us were caught, and brought back to the house by some interfering do-gooders."

"Let me guess," chirped Nina. "You were the one to escape."

"I escaped going back to the house, but I had not evaded the gaze of someone whose eyes had been on me all the time."

"*Mariana.*"

"Correct. She told me she could not resist me, someone as angelic looking as I was. So she decided not to kill me there and then, especially when I told her I was looking for my mother. Though I was lost, confused and more than a little bit frightened. She told me it would only hurt a little."

Nina was a keen observer of Juliana. The vampire looked towards the window, and held her head in her hands.

"It hurt a lot, didn't it?" said Nina, but there was no nastiness in her voice. "Just like it hurt me."

"Yes. It hurt a lot." Juliana ran her hand over the side of her neck. "The wounds have healed on the outside."

"But they never will on the inside," finished Nina. "Why didn't she want to kill you?"

"She was alone in the Castle, the last of the old order, so she told me. She said she would return for me in five years time, and she was a good as her word. I had grown a little, but not as much as other eleven-year-olds. I had not seen her until that day in the cemetery. The day I did to you, what was done to me."

"With one small difference," said Nina; her words hammering like nails into a coffin. "You drained me to the point of death. You let me live, but you did not let me grow. Because of your actions, I have not grown *at all* in body. But for what I lack there, I improved in mind."

"You're not entirely useless then," said Juliana, with the straightest of faces.

"Enough of your barbs, Juliana. How does the story end?"

"I've told you everything I know."

"Then let me tell you how the story ends," spoke Nina authoritatively. "Do you not understand? You must *kill* Mariana, because she is not your mother, no more than I am your sister. I know how it is done, too. A stake through the heart, followed by the severing of the head from its body. I do not have the strength or the height to do it, but you do, and -"

"Enough! You really are a little girl, in mind and body."

"But I don't pretend to be eighteen, as you do. That body is just a shell. *A lie*. But it can do what needs to be done."

"Don't be so stupid, Nina. By her blood we were made, by her undoing we would become undone. We would die."

"At least we would be free of *this*. What is the point of immortality if we must feed like sewer rats?"

"Be quiet! You tire me, Nina, and I have a headache. I need to feed again, even if your pious self does not!"

Juliana elected to end the conversation there, and stormed off in the direction of another room. Nina was not quite finished.

"Juliana! One day, you and your *mother* may see the town repopulated, but you will make mistakes again. They won't come with fire next time, but stakes, and they will cut your angelic looking head off, and impale it on that church's spire for all to see! They'll-"

There was a loud knock at the door, and even Juliana's footsteps, which could be heard by no-one around for miles except for Nina, refrained from making any more sound on the stone floor.

"Who is it, Nina? We expect no-one at the castle. If it someone who is lost, by all means, let them in. After listening to all your wittering, I need fresh blood. Let them in!"

Nina unbolted the huge door, and effortlessly pulled it back. Standing in front of her was a young woman, who was shivering in the cold of the night.

"I'm so sorry to trouble you, but the weather has made a turn for the worse, and I need shelter. Please, please don't turn me away."

Nina tried to implore the woman to go, and not only that, but run like the Devil was behind her. She was fearful Juliana would kill her, though Nina would have admitted to recognising the scent of the woman's blood. Its power, its pull, was overwhelming. Still, Nina found it within herself to resist.

"I am sorry, we do not have any room here. You should leave."

The woman looked at Nina so strangely. In her head, she commended the young girl for seeing right through her. It was obvious this woman was not lost, or cold. She appeared to be here on some kind of mission, and would not be deterred.

"Nina, what in the world are you doing? Please be more courteous to strangers in future!"

Extending her hand to the woman, who misread the intention and handed Juliana her hat and scarf, Juliana smiled sheepishly and invited her in.

"What a night," said the woman. "It is quite brutal out there. If you had not answered, I am sure I would have perished. Thank you, thank you so much for your kindness."

Juliana hung up the woman's clothing, and smiled at Nina, who did not smile back.

"Nina, it is late. You can go for your rest now. I will tend to our guest."

"If it's all the same, I should like to stay," replied Nina. She would not be happy for this woman to be left alone with Juliana. Nina felt she would be in mortal danger.

"It's *not* all the same, Nina. You may go now."

The woman said nothing whilst Juliana and Nina traded glares. In the end, Nina decided to go, but only as far as the room next to Juliana. Nina expected Juliana would take the woman there, and do *the deed*.

As she went to the adjoining bedroom, thoughts raced through her head. Nina patiently waited for Juliana to bring the woman through. It was unlikely she would kill her in the great hall or the dining area. No doubt Mariana would chastise her for making a mess, and if Nina knew one thing about Juliana – she did not like being reprimanded.

After a very short conversation, Nina could make out the muffled sounds of the two women going into the bedroom. Nina wondered when she would have to make a move. She could not let Juliana ruthlessly kill her. The woman had only been looking for shelter, after all.

Or had she?

Just what was this woman up to? If she knew what Juliana was, she would not go anywhere near her, surely?

Nina decided she would wait five minutes, but not a second more.

In the next bedroom, the lights were dimmed, curtains fully drawn. Rich velvet drapes adorned the walls. The bed was huge, but looked almost too grand, and even though it must have been many years since its first construction, it had hardly been used.

Still, Juliana sat the woman down.

"Welcome to our humble abode. My name is Juliana. Here, you can rest. *You'll have an excellent sleep, I'm sure.* I'll take my leave of you now."

"Oh no," said the woman. "Have I done something to offend you? I was hoping you might stay awhile."

"Alright then, I will!" Having had enough of preppy Nina, Juliana seemed happy for company closer to her own age.

The woman produced a bottle of wine from her bag, set it down on the dresser, and reached for two glasses.

"Oh no," said Juliana. "I do not drink wine. It upsets my stomach and gives me headaches."

"When it is produced for the many, not the few. But not this wine. Won't you try some?"

The woman seemed insistent, but Juliana was even more insistent. She would not drink something she had not prepared with her own hands.

"It was just that you seemed nervous," smiled the woman. "I wanted to put you at ease. After all, you have given me shelter, and I am grateful."

Juliana was not in the mood for a kill, although letting the woman go would be a waste. She decided to take her leave, and would return to her coffin. She would kill her in the morning. Such a fine specimen of womanhood would be wasted on the likes of Nina, who wouldn't know what to do with her anyway.

"I've been rude. I don't even know your name," said Juliana.

"My name is Annabelle," said the woman, who uncorked the bottle and was not at all surprised when Juliana caught the cork, but gave the impression she was. "Now we know each other's names, won't you stay with me?"

Okay. It will have to be done tonight then, thought Juliana, who did all she could to prevent her fangs from showing.

***

Next door, Nina was anything but asleep. That young woman was
in mortal danger. Nina lay on her bed, then stood up, only to sit
down again. There was nothing she could do to stop Juliana killing
the woman. *If only I had not opened the door*, thought Nina
ruefully.

She decided to act, even if it made Juliana upset. *Very upset.*

***

She left the room silently, and looked through the keyhole to the
bedroom, which of course, Juliana had locked from the inside. Not
a problem for Nina to enter, but it would be a problem should the
woman wish to leave. Juliana would rip her apart before letting that
happen.

Nina looked through the keyhole on her tiptoes. She hated being so
short. If ever there was a time to change form, this was it. But Nina
wanted to save the woman from a certain and brutal death – she
would need all her energy for that.

Nina wished there was some way to reach Juliana, and get through
to her. Still, from what she observed, the woman did not appear
nervous. Juliana, who was used to being in control of proceedings,
looked to be the nervous one.

The woman looked towards the door, and Nina's balance wobbled.
Had she been seen? She could not tell for sure.

The woman was sipping a red wine from her glass. Juliana did not trust anyone, and never let her guard down, but it appeared that this woman, who was rather attractive, seemed to be beguiling Juliana. "Are you sure you won't have some?" asked the woman, whose demeanour had changed so much from the nervous stranger who knocked at the door of the castle.

She flicked her long brown hair, and lay back on the bed. Nina knew the format – it would not be long now.

"I'll have some," said Juliana, the chill in the room dropping as she spoke. "Some of *you*."

"I was hoping you'd say that," gave the woman as her reply.

Nina could not believe the woman was showing no fear. *Unless she was a vampire herself! Maybe she is here to kill Juliana and me,* thought Nina. *Good, because it means Juliana will die first.*

Juliana didn't waste time, and targeted the woman's neck. For her own part, the woman appeared to place a kiss of her own on the vampire's neck. Juliana screamed – no – it was more like a howl, and Nina had to close her hands over her ears. What was going on?

"Child! Are you there?" shouted the woman known as Annabelle. "Come in if you are. Get in here now!"

If anything, Nina found herself to be more unnerved by the turn of events. She did not trust Juliana, but whoever, or whatever this woman was, one thing was certain. She was not to be a willing victim of Juliana.

Juliana placed a hand over her neck, but it was useless. Her skin felt like it was on fire. Annabelle had not bitten her, but the liquid from her lips had made contact with the vampire's skin, which turned from dead cold to the hottest fire.

As she burned, Nina actually started to feel sorry for Juliana.

"Child! You are there, I know you are. Come in now. I know you can do that. *Come on!*"

Nina did not necessarily act on what the woman said. She just had an overwhelming urge to go to Juliana, whose beauty was deserting her. Her luscious red hair fell in clumps to the floor, her hands wrinkled, and her face darkened as whatever could be called *life*, left her.

"What is going on? Who are you?" demanded Nina.

"First things first, child. Get a knife. A large one, about eight inches to the blade. Now."

Nina rushed from the room, to the main dining area, and grabbed a knife almost too large for her hands. As she ran back to where Juliana appeared to be dying, she did not know if she would give it to this Annabelle. She might have to try and kill this woman herself.

Holding the blade with the point towards the woman, Nina, who had her self-preservation in mind, asked her, "Are you here to kill me too? What have you done to her?"

Annabelle laughed. "No, child. I am here to *save* you. As for that creature, it has been touched by the Blood of Christ. Now, little one – strike her head from her shoulders."

Nina's hands shook. She felt terror, remorse, confusion all at the same time. Many times she had wanted this, the sight of Juliana dying. But now the moment was here, she felt sorry for the girl.

"If you cannot do, what needs to be done, give the knife to me, and I will do it."

"Who *are* you?" demanded Nina.

"I am a nun from the convent. The priest was attacked, probably by this creature. If we do not destroy it, the priest will become one of the undead. Child, I will not let that happen. This creature must die if you are to be free of her."

Nina could not believe her ears. It was surely fantasy that the one that made you a vampire, once killed, held no power over you, providing you had not killed yourself. This would be Nina's only chance. A chance to see her mother again. It could not be passed up. Juliana was suffering, and in Nina's view, it was no more than she deserved. She had to do this for Juliana's sake.

"Let me go to her. Please!" cried Nina.

Annabelle calmly left the room. Once Nina had entered, the lock was no longer secure.

"No mercy, child. By the time I have retrieved my coat and *wimple*, I hope you will have done, what needs to be done."

So that's what it was. Juliana was so excited to see fresh blood that she had not checked what the woman had handed to her.

As she walked, Nina wasted little time. Even before Annabelle had collected her belongings, she heard a sound which sounded as if Juliana had finally been put to rest.

A scream more like a wolf's howl, emanating from Nina appeared to have confirmed this state of affairs.

Annabelle returned to the room.

"Child, is it done? The evil one is dead?"

"Come have a look for yourself."

But there was hardly any need to step into the room. Juliana had returned to her angelic looking self, and her body lay still. Nina was covered in blood, blotches of red all over her dress. The decapitation of Juliana had spilled so much blood that Nina's arms dripped with blood, and some had even splashed onto her face.

Annabelle realised that Nina had executed a tremendous act, and yet had feelings for the monster. Nina lay her head on Juliana's chest, blood seeping into her black hair.

"Come with me to the convent, little one. You can do no more here. Let her be at peace. What is your name?"

"Nina."

"Well Nina, you have done the town a great service this day."

"How so?"

"Well, by killing the one who harmed you."

"Oh. I haven't done that."

"What? No, child, you misunderstand me."

"No," said Nina, shaking her head. "You misunderstand *me*."

"What?"

Nina cleared up the misunderstanding, by turning around sharply, and plunged the knife into Annabelle's stomach. In order to fool the nun, Nina had simply covered herself in Juliana's blood, and the plan had worked.

Juliana raised slowly from the floor, and savaged the nun's body until there was very little left. Nina covered her eyes from the terrible image, but she could still hear Juliana enjoying herself.

"You had your chance, Nina. Why didn't you take it?" asked Juliana.

"When it came to it, I couldn't do it. Better the devil you know, isn't that how the saying goes?"

"Lucky for me then. It looks like you and I have an understanding, little Nina."

"An understanding, yes. But I have killed now, and my innocence is forever lost." She sighed, her heart heavy with remorse. "Will you be alright?"

"I've had worse." Juliana's attempt to cheer Nina up had fallen flat on its face. "Be happy, Nina. Your obsession with innocence, should you wish to retain it, is completely assured. It wasn't you that took her life - *I did,* okay? You can sleep in total peace at night."

"Well, she may not be the last to try to kill us. She mentioned a priest, one who is recovering at the convent. Was it you? Did you attack him?"

"What? He's with the nuns at the convent?" asked Juliana, with surprise and a hint of delight in her voice.

"So she says."

"*Said*, not says," corrected Juliana. "She's dead now. She doesn't say anything anymore."

Deciding to finally put aside their differences and mutual distrust of each other, Juliana hugged Nina towards her.

"You've done great tonight, Nina. The priest – *and* the nuns – are the least of our worries."

Sleep, Little Darling

N ina had not given up on seeing her mother again. She had

decided that having Juliana on her side was better than constantly behaving like they were enemies. Besides, Juliana seemed to have genuinely changed since being attacked by the nun formerly known as Annabelle.

Nina would join Juliana on increasingly frequent visits to the town, which had grown in its population once more. The horrors of the Blood and the Raven had seemingly been forgotten. At the very least, people would deny anything bad had happened in the town, fearing that visitors from afar would bypass the place, and along with them would go much needed money for the area.

As for what happened to those who had massacred the previous population, Juliana had told Nina that those particular vampires had left the town, and gone to spread their terror to others.

The nun had made a grave error, thinking that Juliana was the head vampire. She had paid the ultimate price for her mistake.

The case to kill Mariana became stronger by the day.

The experience with the nun was perhaps Nina's destiny. Juliana had previously thought Nina far too weak and conflicted to ever carry out a kill. But things had changed for them both, perhaps forever.

Juliana's influence had not been completely lost on Nina, who began to practise different forms on a regular basis. She decided to practise on her own. Nina did not want to give Juliana any other thought than she would be a compliant, well-behaved and dutiful vampire.

Today's form was *mist*. This was the one Nina seemed to have the most trouble with. Juliana had described it as simply 'letting go', and it really did feel like every part of her body was not just being pulled apart, but actually falling apart. Not a comfortable feeling at all.

Nina found she could only hold the form for a few seconds at first, but it was getting easier with practise.

Taking the form of the raven, a kind of perverted inspiration from Mariana, was something Nina could do, but was very unhappy with. She felt rather small and vulnerable. It might be fun for the adult vampires to morph into a much smaller form, but as Nina was small already, she wanted to experiment with larger targets.

She was not envious of Juliana, but she did like her figure. Whilst she had been tired, and surprisingly so, from turning into mist, transforming herself into an adult female was much easier.

Nina looked at her figure in the mirror, which gave off a faint reflection, and realised she could try on some of Juliana's adult dresses after all.

She rushed to the wardrobe, and defiantly chose one of the imperial yellow coloured dresses.

The dress felt good, and real enough, because of course it *was* real. Her body, although pleasing to the eye, was a little less curvaceous than Juliana's, and for that matter, was not as tall as Mariana either. The body felt hollow. A shell. Nina looked again and again at herself. She loved what she could see, but not what she could feel. She wanted to ask Juliana just one thing – is it possible for a vampire to truly enjoy this existence, when, in her mind, it felt anything but real.

It was likely Juliana would just laugh at her, and say *You're dead, you stupid little girl. Be glad you've got this existence. You see the world like no-one else does. Why don't you just enjoy it?*

Apart from appearing to wrestle with her conscience in the small hours, Juliana genuinely seemed to get a kick out of being a vampire.

"When you're not suffering from amnesia, you bitch!" screamed Nina, she had thought to no-one in particular.

"Just what do you think you're doing?" Juliana had returned, unbeknownst to Nina.

"I'm-I'm-I-" Nina stammered.

Juliana stood in front of Nina, glaring at her. "Well?"

"I was just wanting to know, what it was like. But it's a game. A stupid game. Who am I kidding? I'll never be like you."

To Nina's surprise, Juliana's stern expression softened. Nina thought that this might be the kind of situation where sisters would hug, but Juliana could be relied upon to keep her distance.

"I heard what you said, you know," said Juliana, but there was no obvious hatred in her tone. "I'm not amnesic; it is just easier to block out those things. You'll learn why I do that, when you make your first kill. A vampire cannot have a conscience."

"You're still on about that. You'll never let it go, will you?"

"You can wear that dress whenever you like, once you have done what you need to do."

It never failed to both surprise and unsettle Nina how Juliana could change from menacing, to pleasant, back to being menacing once more. She desired the adult form no longer, and morphed back into her small body.

"You're taller than I was when I was your age. Best get the dress off, Nina. I don't want you dragging the hem on the floor, making it all dirty."

"Have your bloody dress then!"

Nina stormed off in a huff to her bedroom, and ignored Juliana's attempts at reconciliation. Nina was tired of Juliana's behaviour, whose mood seemed to swing in the direction the wind happened to blow.

She slept for a while, then, when she woke, she had an inspirational thought. A way to save herself, and Juliana. She would need outside help for this, so as the light escaped from the sky, she prepared to meet the one who could make it happen.

***

Nina took a deep breath, and opened the window in her bedroom. A strong wind buffeted the castle. Just for a moment, her footing was unsure, and her confidence wavered in what she was about to do. She looked down but could not see the bottom, for she was high up in the castle grounds.

Attempting to regain her composure, she swung a foot off the ledge, but immediately pulled it back. She doubted a vampire could die from jumping from a height, but wanted to know, all the same. Perhaps she was more human than she believed. Save for her appearance, Juliana was anything but human. Any being that came into contact with her, would find that out at their cost. But for Nina, this life, this existence, whatever it was, and regardless of what Juliana called it, was not for her.

So she jumped.

Was it true, or a trick of the mind, that when someone faces death, that your life flashes before you? Nina could see her mother. She recalled an early memory of her mother in her police officer's uniform.

She recalled playing at school, wearing her own dresses. Not a care in the world.

Another memory. One where Marcus and Rocco casually walked into the school, and walked hand in hand with Nina, saying they had been sent by her mother to collect her, and had told the teachers that they were good friends with *Occifer* O'Hara.

Oh, Nina could remember it all so clearly. An innocent time, before she was made into a vampire. Marcus and Rocco had tied her up and left her all alone in the cemetery chapel. She screamed, they told her to shut up. Marcus even slapped her, the sting on her cheeks only slightly calmed by the tears from her eyes.

"It's you or us," Marcus told the very frightened young girl, "and it is not going to be *us*."

Just before she hit the ground, Nina remembered the last sentence from her captors, when the younger looking one asked if it would work. "It had better, otherwise we'll all be dead."

Nina was just a few feet from the ground, before timing her transformation to perfection.

A small vampire bat she was, but one that was able to fly nonetheless. It had been easier to fly when Mariana and Juliana had been ahead of her, but now Nina would have to manage this herself. She needed help, and whilst Mariana existed, there would be no saving her, nor freedom for Juliana, who simply and ruthlessly carried out her *mother's* wishes.

Nina would not enter via the front door. This was to be no quiet entry. It was a risk, but one she had to take. Her descent through the top window of the convent was met with a loud crash that shattered the peaceful night.

The glass was everywhere, but as Nina transformed into her true shape, the nuns who ran into the room to see what had happened could only look on in wonder at first, before the adrenaline kicked in; and the only emotion they could feel, was *fear*.

"Child of Satan! Stay back!" screamed one of the nuns. She brandished a cross at Nina, who hissed, and the cross burned the nun's hand, forcing her to drop it.

"I'm here to help," said Nina sternly. "The priest – where is he? Where are you keeping him?"

The nuns looked at each other, with one of them, perhaps a Sister, shook her head as if to instruct them not to speak. Nina wasted no further time and grabbed the Sister by her throat.

"Alright then – you think having one of us here is bad? Wait until the lot of you are *Children of Satan*. Now take me to him if you want to live."

One of the nuns shrieked as Nina ripped her habit from her shoulders.

"For *my* protection," said Nina. "Your blasted crosses are everywhere."

It was much worse than that for Nina. She felt so weak, diseased by the convent, just as the church had weakened her. The only thing going for her, was that she had not killed. In the end, would their God take pity on her black soul?

She scrubbed such thoughts from her head. This was no longer about her, but about everyone. She could not kill Mariana without help, and Juliana, perhaps understandably, had refused. If the priest turned into a vampire, he would kill all the nuns too. That would be the kindest thing to do for them. Still, while he lived, there was hope.

The nuns instructed Nina to walk down an ever-winding staircase, its walls were narrow, its steps even more narrow and steep. Nina decided not to use her powers to glide, and walked as the humans did.

Finally, they entered a great hall, but it was shrouded in darkness. Ahead of Nina was an altar, and sure enough, the priest lay on top of it. She knew it was him, even though his body was covered with a sheet, which was purple in colour.

His hand lay to the side, draped over the edge of the altar. Nina recognised the small purple birthmark on the priest's hand. It was unmistakable. This had to be him. She could sense he was still breathing. Some of the nuns began to sob and whimper.

"Cut that out, will you?" snapped Nina. "It would seem I am not the only child around here."

Nina pulled back the sheet. The priest was weak, but certainly alive. He tried to say something, but it was barely a whisper. Nina smiled as he heard his words.

"You can't seem to keep yourself away from these holy places, can you child?"

"That depends on what you term as *holy*, isn't it Father?"

"What do you want, child?"

"The same as you. An end to the Dreymuirs."

"You lie."
Nina pressed a nail into her wrist, and turned her hand over. The nuns screamed as blood splattered onto the priest's mouth.

"I don't care if you think I am telling the truth or not. I don't have time for this and-"

Nina turned the priest's head to the side. The marks of the vampire lay on his neck, but they were not clean. It was as if a beast had made them. The puncture wounds looked unclean, sore and angry. Even if the nuns had tried to clean the wounds up, their ministrations had only served to make things considerably worse.

"-neither do you, *priest*."

The priest attempted to spit the blood out, but Nina pinched his nose and held his mouth open. "By her blood we are made, by the spilling of her blood will we become undone."

Nina turned her attention to the nuns. "All of you stay back, if you know what's good for you. He is weak. I am just trying to strengthen him for this task."

"What task?" screamed one of the nuns. "We will not let you take him to the castle to be sacrificed."

"Fine," said Nina, who wiped a bloody hand on the purple cloth. "You can wait for Mariana and her delightful daughter to come here. Then you'll be the ones being sacrificed."

"Wicked child!" screamed the Sister. "You will burn in Hell!"

"Oh Sister, don't be so obtuse. *I am already there*."
"Yes, Sister, leave her be. This is the child's day off."

The priest had recovered quickly. Enough to speak clearly, and to stand unaided.

"Father, no." The Sister spoke sorrowfully. "The child is evil."

"Maybe she is, maybe she isn't," replied the priest, who could feel the blood of Nina and Juliana coursing through his veins. "She came here tonight at great risk to herself. I will go with her and do what needs to be done."

The nuns reluctantly stood aside and watched as the priest and the little girl vampire walked slowly in the direction of the castle.

"Sister, as soon as dawn has broken, make the call to the Bishop," spoke one of the nuns. "I expect that the church will be needing a new parish priest."

***

"Are you *scared*, Father?" asked Nina.

"No, child. The Lord gives me strength."

"Which Lord would that be?"

The priest smiled. "I am not playing this game with you. Satan is alive within you, child."

"So you walk with the Devil, just as Jesus did for forty days and forty nights. As the raven flies, we will walk for less than forty minutes, Father. Perhaps the Lord *does* give you strength. You're going to need it."

As they walked towards the castle, Nina explained what needed to be done, and the order in which these actions were to be carried out. The bodies of Juliana and Mariana Dreymuir would be in their respective coffins. If one were attacked, and killed, the other would attack her assailant. It would not be possible for Nina to kill both at the same time.

"I'm quick, but not that quick Father. You will stake Mariana through the heart. I will take care of Juliana."

"It should be the other way around. You are making this too personal, child."

"Juliana spilled my blood. I am merely returning the favour."

Cries of *Jesus Christ* filled the air.

"Father, you're not trying to attract attention, are you? I need you focussed for this."

"What will happen after we have driven stakes through their hearts?"

"I'm pretty curious to find out, Father."

Another *Jesus Christ.*

"This is not a game, child!"

"I'm glad we're singing from the same hymn sheet," smiled Nina.
"You see, Father? I can make jokes too."

***

As they turned up the road, the sky seemed to turn even blacker in
colour. The moon shone brightly, almost lighting a trail for them to
follow to the Castle.

The gates swung open, the creaking sound alarmed the priest,
whose head had began to swim with feelings of evil so
overwhelming, he wanted to lift the little girl up and impale her
body on the gate.

He gripped his left wrist with his hand, and prayed to God that he
would get a hold of himself. The girl was right. The Dreymuirs had
to die, and although they too would almost certainly die, at least
this line of vampires would be at an end.

"Any questions before we go in?" asked Nina.

"Just the one. *How* have you fought the urge to kill?"

"It has taken more strength than you will ever fully understand,
Father. Maybe one day, you will know what I've gone through."

187

"Then let us get it over with, and be done with it," said the priest solemnly.

Nina told the priest to walk to the north part of the Castle.
"I have to get the stakes," said, Nina. "*Go*. I will catch up with you in a moment."
The priest sensed Nina was leading him into a trap, but said nothing of his concerns. If it come to it, he would kill three vampires tonight, before throwing himself down onto the spikes below. He promised himself that no matter what happened on this night, he would not become one of them.

Sure enough, he entered the darkened mausoleum. It was deathly quiet. He counted more than three coffins, which started the nerves once again. The priest had a nervous tick in his left cheek, and right now, it was doing overtime.

As he approached the coffins, it was obvious to him which ones contained Mariana and Juliana Dreymuir. Where the dust had been disturbed, the coffin lids were shiny. Others remained completely covered in dust, as if it were a second skin.

"Or a *shroud*. That's what you were thinking, right Father?" Nina had returned with two sharpened stakes, each one as big as she was.

"You just have to place your hand on the coffin lid, and it will rise," instructed Nina, her voice barely audible. "Don't try and heave it open, as humans do. You no longer possess human strength. But if your Lord gives you strength, use it to bury that stake into Mariana's chest. You must also use *this*."

Nina produced a dagger and gave it to him. "After you've staked her, hold her head up like this-"

Nina raised her own head up by pulling on her hair.

"- then use the blade to take the head clean off. Don't second guess yourself, Father."

"That I won't, child. That I won't."

Nina touched the coffin lid containing Juliana, who slept with her hands resting on her chest.

"See how I did it, Father? See how the casket opens?"

The priest nodded that he understood. "She looks like an angel, child. Not at all like the vile creature that has killed so many."

"Yes. She looks so innocent while she sleeps, Father. But I tell you, she does not rest. Her conscience does not allow her. The faces of everyone she has killed torments her. For my own part, I start to pity her. I no longer hate her. Finally, I can give her peace tonight. Are you ready, Father?"

The priest replied with a yes, but as he approached the coffin containing Mariana Dreymuir, a great and terrible fear washed over him. He could not grip his hand this time, because he carried a stake in his right hand, and a dagger in the other.

He took one more look at Nina, who was shaking, but was prepared to do what needed to be done. She held the stake high above her head, preparing to bring it down on Juliana.

The delay was enough for Mariana, whose eyes opened as the priest stood in front of her coffin.

Over at the other casket, Nina cried out as she brought the stake down. Blood splashed everywhere, spilling over the coffin. Juliana's eyes flashed open as her dress was stained with blood.

Nina looked strange, just like the first time Juliana had observed her, just before she had plunged her fangs deep into the little girl's neck.

Whilst still holding the stake above her head, Nina looked down towards her chest, which had a blade sticking out from it. She realised that it was her own blood that had been spilled, not Juliana's.

From just a few feet away, Nina could make out another voice.

"Good work, Father. You see, Juliana? I *told* you she would betray us!"

Mariana kept her glare on the priest, who forcibly removed the blade from Nina's back.

Nina stumbled, and began to lose her balance. Nina had time to see a bloodied but triumphant Juliana emerge from her coffin. Just before she collapsed on the floor, blood flowed without restriction from Nina's body.

Juliana crouched over Nina, then cradled her head in her hands.

"I did what had to be done," said the priest, who was still affected by Mariana's gaze.

"Yes, you did Father," said Mariana. "Yes you did."

"Now I've got to do, what I've got to do," said Juliana.

"My eyes, my sight has darkened, *Julie*," said Nina listlessly.
"I know," said Juliana. "Father, give me that blade, will you?"

"Julie. Did all our talk mean nothing at all to you?" asked Nina.

"Not *all* of it," said Juliana, as she pressed the blade to Nina's throat.

"I thought…I thought you told me vampires don't kill each other."

"Sorry about that, Nina. I lied."

"I know," she replied softly.

"You want peace? You want to see your mother again?"

"I do. Mother, I'll see you again. I'll see-"

Juliana screamed in silence as she took the girl's head off cleanly.

Mariana leaned back on Juliana's open coffin. She had kept her cold-eye glaze on the priest the entire time.

She wrapped a cold arm around him, and gestured to Juliana, who was still holding the blade, to stand up. Juliana forced herself to smile as she complied, but she expected the face of Nina would haunt her until her final moments.

Juliana addressed the priest one final time, as the gleam of the blade was clotted with Nina's blood.

"Well Father, what shall we do with you?"

Author Reflections

I experienced a lot of conflict when writing this story, as the death of Nina is something I found rather troubling. In a way, she experiences death twice – only this time, it will be the end for her. At least she can find peace at long last.

Perhaps even more troubling is how Juliana's story ends in this book. She is a vampire who spreads great terror to those she encounters, but she returns to being compliant and dutiful when Mariana is around.

It's possible that Juliana would have been grateful to Nina. But once Mariana put the priest under her spell, using the Medusa-like gaze upon him, Nina is doomed.

I always try to keep readers guessing, which is never easy. It would have made sense for Nina and the priest to destroy Juliana and Mariana, but what then?

The priest had been weakened by Mariana, only to be further strengthened by Nina. When he stabs Nina through her back, was he merely attacking the vampire that was closest to him, or deciding to get rid of Nina so that Juliana and Mariana would spare his life, such as it was?

Readers will make up their own mind. In my view, Nina had a noble aim in trying to rid the world of Juliana and Mariana. Once Nina had learned that other vampires were in other towns, the only way to stop the spread was to kill the head vampire.

If Mariana has previously spoken the truth, that she has existed for as long as God has been around, then she had a power that was so terrible if she were to wield it, an entire civilisation could be enslaved.

I don't think Mariana wants that kind of attention. She still wants to see Marcus and Rocco again, even if they don't want to reciprocate.

For Juliana, deep within her lies one last part of humanity. She does have a conscience, which is why she is rather sad, in the end, about having to destroy Nina.

No doubt, Mariana would not have it any other way.

- John Hennessy, February 2015

By the same Author

Dream the Crow's Black Dream
A Tale of Vampires: Book Four

Several years have passed since Seth McAndrew was forced to recount the tale of The Blood and the Raven.

Now, on one of the most important days in his life, the sadistic vampire he thought had been buried along with his past, makes a very unwelcome return.

When he refuses to succumb to her violent and disturbing needs, the body count ruthlessly and rapidly increases. Seth realises with brutal clarity that he cannot escape the curse of the vampire.

An opportunity arises when he meets another of her kind. Piece by piece, a recurring dream shows him how he might just put an end to her killing ways. But will he be prepared to risk the best thing in his life, in order to destroy the worst?

Dark Winter: The Wicca Circle

Romilly Winter is no ordinary heroine, just a reluctant one.

She has a gift. She can see the future. But can she see far enough? The world in which she lives is under attack – the dead are rising, and evil follows her at every turn.

Will she be able to save herself – and the world?"

From the Diary of Romilly Winter, October 14th.

"I've had two years to prepare for this. In that time, I have never told a soul. Of course, my Nan knew. She'd bequeathed me the mirror, after all. Now, maybe tonight, tomorrow, in a few days, the event that I don't want to happen with all my heart, will come to pass. I'm not ready. I know I'm not ready, and yet, it will happen nonetheless.

Nan had this thing in her possession for nearly seventy years. She had told me I simply had to be at Rosewinter, prior to my sixteenth birthday no matter what objections my parents raised. She said I was 'special', and was the only one equipped to deal with what was coming.

The problem is, I don't feel special, I just feel…different, and in all probability, that isn't going to be good enough.

In just two days time, I will be sixteen years old, and if anything my Nan said is remotely true, I will be lucky to survive that long…."

Dark Winter: Crescent Moon

The second story in the Dark Winter trilogy.

Murderous Little Darlings
A Tale of Vampires Series: Book One

Three siblings. An endless list of victims. A whole lot of time to
kill.

With two specimens of the undead on either side of her, Juliana
knew there was no escape. Kill the one they had selected for her, or
be killed, and become one of them. What had the neighbours in the
road called them, back when their childhood pranks were just that?

Oh yes, she remembered now. Murderous Little Darlings. They had
the faces of angels, but possessed the very soul of the Devil.

Marcus had fully embraced his vampire side from the moment he
was born. Rocco was the second eldest, and had fought the
temptation all of his life. Then Marcus finally broke him.

That just left Juliana. Will she resist them, or join in the hunt?

The Blood and the Raven

A Tale of Vampires Series: Book Two

A group of teenagers spend a night amongst the ruins of an old priory, taking turns to scare one other with a tale of horror, each one more scary than the last.

When it comes to Seth, the last storyteller, he is reluctant to tell the story, because once the tale has been told, those who hear it, will begin to die.

His friends think Seth is bluffing - but is he in fact, telling the truth?

To find out, you must dare to read the tale of The Blood and The Raven.

Innocent While She Sleeps

A Tale of Vampires Series: Book Three

Tormented by all the wicked and evil deeds she has committed in her life, Juliana has never known what it is like to truly rest in peace. Far from the confines of the Blood and the Raven; at Castle Dreymuir, a most unlikely source offers her a way out of the life.

Initially, Juliana dismisses it out of hand; stating the cost is far too high for her to possibly consider. But as time goes on, one overwhelming desire eats away at her - a return to innocence in both her waking hours and whilst she sleeps.

Will Juliana accept this deadly but most compelling of offers, so that she can put her deadly existence to rest, once and for all?

Clara's Song

Be careful what you wish for.

Clara Bayliss dreams of escaping her boring marriage. When her car fails to start after a freakish accident, her fantasy has every chance of becoming the reality.

Rescued by the very man she thought had been killed, she takes a ride into the unknown with him, and has no intention of returning home.

Her husband isn't pleased about being dumped. Especially when he finds out the news she's been keeping from him.And then, there's a song, the one that Clara would play whenever she needed freeing from a world full of despair.

Clara's Song.
It would make her feel good. Strong. Independent. Fearless.
Only…her rescuer knows the song too, and for him, it means something else entirely…

A dark, psychotic tale of lost dreams and total paranoia from which there is no escape.

Dark Winter: Last Rites

Coming 2016 - The final story in the Dark Winter trilogy.

If you enjoyed reading this book, please consider leaving a review on Amazon.com and / or the country's website where you obtained the book.

I'll be announcing a new website very soon, so to keep up to date, please send me your email so you can be added to the list. You can contact me at authorjohnhennessy@yahoo.com

Don't forget that Book Four – Dream the Crow's Black Dream is available for purchase now:-
http://www.amazon.com/Dream-Crows-Black-Tale-Vampires-ebook/dp/B00U57JWZM/ref=sr_1_1?s=books&ie=UTF8&qid=1436551480&sr=1-1&keywords=dream+the+crow%27s+black+dream

The fifth book in the series, *Reunion of the Blood*, will be released in early 2016.

Thank you for taking the time to read my work.

Printed in Great Britain
by Amazon.co.uk, Ltd.,
Marston Gate.